Has Anyone Seen Alice?

By

P. T. CHAMBERS

*To Ellie
With best wishes
Philip xx*

ISBN 978-0-9935923-1-7

Copyright © 2016 P.T. Chambers

Revised edition. All rights reserved. No parts of this publication "Has Anyone Seen Alice?" may be reproduced, stored in a retrieval system or transmitted in any form or by any means, without the prior written permission of the author, nor be otherwise circulated in any form of binding or cover other than that in which it is published and without a similar condition being imposed by the purchaser.

This book is intended for your personal enjoyment only. All characters in this publication are fictitious and any resemblance to any person living or dead is purely coincidental. Published in Ireland by Orla Kelly Publishing. Proofread by Red Pen Edits.

Dedication

To Margaret

Acknowledgements

Big thanks to Margaret for giving me the space to live for long periods in my imagination. A special thanks to both my immediate and extended families for their absolute belief that I could write a book and for their continual encouragement.

A special word of thanks for my friends John Quinn, Brian Fitzgerald, and Dominic Martin who edited the book for me with such enthusiasm. Without their honesty and expertise, this book would never have been written.

Thanks also to Kevin Murphy and Lorraine Griffin for setting up my blog.

Finally, a special thanks to Orla Kelly, Orla Kelly Self-Publishing Services, who introduced me to the world of Self-Publishing and put it all together.

About The Author

Phil Chambers (P.T. Chambers) grew up in Cork City, Ireland and is the founding member of the Business Analysts Association of Ireland. Having spent a lifetime working in the business community, Phil also finds time for sport, hillwalking, music, reading and gardening.

Phil began writing a little over two years ago and since then has had a number of short stories published.

He blogs at ramblingsfromphilc.blogspot.ie and he can be contacted at ptchambers@eircom.net.

His sequel 'Retribution for Alice' takes up where 'Has Anyone Seen Alice?' ends.

*"Oh what a tangled web we weave
when first we practice to deceive."*
Sir Walter Scott

Has Anyone Seen Alice?

Chapter 1

According to the latest polls, Gregg Newman was a certainty to become the city's next mayor. With three weeks to go to polling day, the opinion polls showed him a massive fourteen points ahead of his nearest rival, Mark Swanson. The bookies had closed their books on Newman and were only open for bets on the other candidates. That was if anyone was foolish enough to do so, or just believed in miracles.

Gregg Newman had everything going for him; good looks, money, an Ivy League education and an impressive law degree behind him. He was his Party's golden boy, destined to use the office of mayor, when he was elected, as a stepping stone to the Senate. After that, who knew where he would end up?

Right now his colleagues in the law firm where he worked, and who were excited about having one of their own being elected as mayor, were trying to convince him to join them in the local hostelry for early Friday evening drinks. However, Newman had promised his eight-year-old daughter, Tracey, whom he adored, that he would be home by seven o'clock, collect her from the neighbor who was minding her, and take her out for some fast food and on to see a film she had been begging him to bring her to. He also had a six o'clock meeting that he didn't intend to miss.

He was acutely aware of the role his colleagues had played four years previously when his career was in tatters, arising out of the episode that had ended with his wife, Alice, being declared insane and committed to a psychiatric facility upstate. Without their support he would not, at forty-five years of age, be on the verge of becoming the most powerful man in the city. He owed them at least one drink and would still be home in time to freshen up before collecting Tracey. After all the film didn't commence until eight thirty.

Almost two hours later, as he drove home along the lake with the street lights reflecting in the still water, he began to consider whether or not he would move to a bigger, and possibly a more centrally located house, when he became mayor of the city. He was still considering his options as he reached the tree lined cul-de-sac, Elm Grove, and turned into the driveway to his house. Once again, he noticed that the security lights were not on outside the house and decided to make an issue of this with the woman who called to clean the house each Friday. This was not the first time that this had happened and he was determined to make sure it would be the last.

Letting himself into the house, he dumped his briefcase on the hall table and was turning to take off his coat when he felt a stabbing pain in his shoulder. Later, when being interview by the police he would say that he became aware of the presence of someone, dressed in black, emerging from behind the front door.

Chapter 2

Detective Eddie McGrane was just putting his jacket on, having tidied up his desk, and was about to head home for a quiet weekend, just another quiet weekend. One of the many he had had since his divorce. The life of a detective didn't gel with his ex-wife. The weather had been glorious all week and he had promised to join his neighbors for a barbeque that evening and had then planned to take a trip to the lake on Saturday to do some fishing with some of his buddies. He was really looking forward to the break after what had been a pretty rotten week. Just then his cell phone rang. He was sorely tempted to ignore it but then you don't ignore your Chief of Police – that is if you want to develop your career.

"Hi Eddie, thank God I got you. We have a situation. A serious one. Get over to 45 Elm Grove immediately and take Detective Maria Diego with you. You will know the house and its owner, and no flashing lights, as we want to keep this one quiet for now. Let me know the outcome when you assess the situation. Oh and by the way – avoid the freeway, there has been a pile-up near Junction 14."

'Christ, that must be Gregg Newman's address,' thought Eddie.

Fifteen minutes later as he pulled into the exclusive cul-de-sac, with its neat rows of autumnal colored sycamore trees, he noticed that the area around the house had already been taped off and two uniformed officers were patrolling the perimeter. He also noted that the forensics' vehicle had arrived. So far there was no identifiable press presence. After parking their car both he and detective Diego, having identified themselves to the officers, entered the house.

"Well, what have we got?" Eddie asked Lenny Bareman from forensics, whom he met in the hall.

"When we arrived we found a young girl in the bedroom who appears to have been strangled and a very distraught and intoxicated middle aged man sitting on the floor beside the bed. In the sitting room we found a Mr Arthur Spinks being questioned by Officer Andy Maguire. Apparently, Mr Spinks found the situation and called it in. He and his wife were babysitting the daughter of this house – Tracey Newman. When she wasn't collected by Mr Newman, as arranged, and as he couldn't get a reply to his phone calls, he walked over to the house, they live just around the corner, and found the front door unlocked. When he got no response to ringing the bell, he went in to find the situation, which he immediately called in."

"And the guy? Has he been identified?"

"Yeah, according to Mr Spinks, he is none other than

Gregg Newman."

"Wow. And has he said anything?"

"Well, I cautioned him that anything he might say could be used in evidence against him, but he seemed to be very confused and kept muttering something about his wife's perfume in the room. He then asked to have his attorney, Al McNally, contacted which Mr Spinks had already done."

"So where is he now?"

"Officer Walt Carter is in the kitchen plying him with coffee."

"Ok, let's have a look at the bedroom, Maria. And just use your eyes. Just let them take in everything at a glance without judgement."

Careful not to interfere with the forensic team, Eddie noted the girl tied on the bed with a belt looped around her neck, her face the face of death. Neatly folded on the chair beside the bed were a man's clothes with the shoes carefully placed under the chair. On the floor beside the bed was a half empty bottle of whiskey. There was no evidence of a struggle. The scene had all the hallmarks of a sex game that went wrong.

Leaving the room, Eddie decided to bring the Chief up to scratch and went out into the hall to make the call.

"Hi Chief, looks like we have a political bombshell on our hands. All the immediate evidence would suggest that Newman was involved in some sort of sex game with a young girl, whom the neighbor identified as the babysitter Newman and his wife used to hire, that went badly wrong. We have a dead girl on our hands and a very disorientated Newman found in his underpants sitting on the floor beside the bed with a half-finished bottle of whiskey by his side. Other than that we are not sure what went on but should know more when the guys from forensics are finished."

"Christ, what a mess. Has Newman said anything?"

"Apparently Officer Andy Maguire, who was first on the scene, spoke to him but other than a muttering that there was an intruder there, he got no sense out of him. Looks like he is either intoxicated or drugged. He has requested that Al McNally, his attorney, be contacted and I have just seen him arrive."

"OK, I'll contact the District Attorney (DA) and see what she advises. I will set up an incident room for 8:00am in the morning and naturally, all leave is suspended. We need to get a handle on this pronto. In the meantime, keep a lid on it and arrange for the usual house-to-house enquiries to be made immediately."

"Hi Maria," said Eddie, "I want you to check outside

to see if there was any sign of a break-in. Then have a word with Mr Spinks. I'm going to have a look at Newman." As he entered the kitchen he found Al McNally bending down trying to get Gregg Newman to focus on him.

"Ah, detective McGrane, we meet again. I sincerely hope my client's rights have not been violated. As you can see, he is in no condition to be questioned. I have called his doctor and an ambulance to have him taken care of. I will let you know when the doctors agree that he has recovered from whatever happened to him. No doubt there is a very simple explanation for this unfortunate tragedy."

"Agreed, but the longer this goes on, Mr McNally, the harder it will be to keep the media out." replied Eddie as he left the room.

"Well, find anything?" Eddie asked as Maria walked into the hallway.

"No sign of a break-in and Mr Spinks confirmed that the door was open when he got here. He also confirmed that the CCTV cameras in the Grove had been giving trouble in the past few months and that the security firm responsible could not find the fault as it was very intermittent."

"OK, let's call it a day and see what the pathologist and forensics tells us in the morning."

Chapter 3

It had been a shitty day for Shirley Green. For two years she had been learning her trade as a cub-reporter at the local NTTV television station, getting the rump end of the pile of news stories. Today she had decided to confront her boss, Butch Collins, and demand that she be given assignments other than quirky stories about pet cats, strange hobbies, fashion shows and the like. The response had been brutal. If you don't like it, leave it. On top of that, her part-time boyfriend, Jeff, had called her to tell her that he and two of his buddies were going fishing for the weekend. What else could happen? She should have listened to her mother. Jeff was no good.

To while away the time and give her time to think, she decided to walk back to her apartment. Having just passed the university she was tempted to call into one of the coffee shops much frequented by students and lecturers alike. However, she didn't feel like sitting on her own on a Friday evening, sipping her Americano, while all around her would be young couples enjoying the beginning of a long hot weekend. It would only emphasize the fact that she was single.

As she approached the turning into Elm Grove, she

noticed that the street had been blocked off by a string of police incident tape. She then became aware that there appeared to be a number of police cars towards the end of the Grove. She knew that she should know who lived on that street but could not remember who it was. Butch would know. Taking out her cell phone she called the office.

"Hi Butch, Shirley here. I'm on my way home and just noticed that Elm Grove is blocked off and there seems to be a number of police cars outside one of the houses, the one at the end of the Grove. I have a vague memory that I should know someone living in that street but can't remember. Funnily enough there are no flashing lights even though I notice that the area outside the house has been taped off as with a crime scene. I see guys in white overalls going in and out of the house."

"Good girl, Shirley. That's where Gregg Newman lives but I'm not sure of his exact address. See what you can find out and in the meantime I will send a camera crew over. There is one in the neighborhood covering the pile-up on the freeway. They should be finished there by now. Keep in contact."

"Excuse me officer, can you tell me what's going on here?" Shirley, in her best girly voice, asked the officer manning the entrance.

"Move along Miss. As you can see the street is blocked off," came the response.

"I can see that officer, but what I would like to know is what has happened here, has Mr Newman taken ill?"

"Who said anything about Mr Newman? And who exactly are you?"

Producing her NTTV identity card with a flourish, as she had seen the established reporters do, she replied, "I'm Shirley Green from NTTV and we are very interested in anything to do with Mr Newman. Now, can you tell me what's going on?"

Just then the NTTV van arrived and within seconds the team had set up their equipment. As the cameraman, Bo Johnson, began focusing in on the general surroundings he said, "OK Shirley, you get fixed up with earphones and Norman will lead you in."

It was happening, her first big break and the anchor man was none other than Norman Wilder. What a break.

"Well," said Shirley as she faced the camera, "We are here in the leafy cul-de-sac called Elm Grove on this beautiful autumn evening, home to the well-known Gregg Newman, whom many believe will be our next mayor. As you can see, the road has been closed off by a barrier and manned by police officers. Further in, if we can get the camera to zoom in, you will see a number of police cars and police officers dressed in their white overalls examining the area around the house."

Just then an ambulance and a black limousine arrived and were let through the barrier. "An ambulance and a black limousine have just arrived now and are pulling up outside the house. Wait, someone has just got out of the limousine. Can you get a shot of that Bo? He appears to be carrying what looks like a doctor's bag."

"Can you tell our viewers what the police are saying, Shirley?" prompted Norman.

"I have tried to get through the barrier but we are not being allowed beyond where we are. The officer manning the barrier has indicated that there has been what he called, a domestic incident. Whatever that means!"

Just then Eddie and his partner Maria walked out the door into the glare of the camera lights. "Christ, what's going on?" said Eddie.

"NTTV are here." said one of the officers.

"That's Detective Eddie McGrane," Norman prompted Shirley on her earphone. "Ask him for a comment, and Bo, try and get a close up of him. His reaction should tell us something."

As Shirley shouted at Eddie, he abruptly turned and re-entered the house. Once inside, he called his boss.

"Hi boss, sorry to bother you again but we have another problem. Don't ask me how they found out, but NTTV are here, and want a comment. It might be a good idea to get someone from public relations (PR) to come down and say something. In the meantime, I will fudge them off with the usual; 'We are still unsure of the details etc. but will make a statement at ten o'clock.' Would you be happy with that?"

"Thanks Eddie. Can you hold on there until I get someone down? Sorry to mess up your weekend, but as the old saying goes, it never rains but it pours."

As Eddie approached the barrier, Shirley introduced herself and her cameraman. "Detective McGrane can you tell our viewers what exactly has happened? Is Gregg Newman injured?"

"Well, at this point in time we are in the early part of the investigation. It appears from what we can gather that an incident has occurred involving a young girl who was visiting the house. You will no doubt appreciate that for operational reasons we can't say much more at this time."

"But what about Gregg Newman?" replied Shirley.

"As I said, we are not in a position to say any more at this time. We will make a statement around about ten p.m. when we should have a clearer picture. The last thing we need is incorrect information going out over the air. Thank you for your cooperation."

With that he walked back to Maria and got into his car.

"OK Shirley, I heard that," came Norman's voice through her earpiece. "Stay there and keep your prime position and film anything of interest. In the meantime, we will put together a short exclusive for the nine o'clock news and come on with a full report for the ten o'clock news; including the live statement promised by the police. Once we break the news every news hack in town will be swarming around the place like bees around honey."

"Bo, keep your eyes on the house and film anybody coming or going. I am going to nose around and see if I can find out anything from the neighbors." said Shirley.

Around the corner of the street there was a coffee shop that Shirley knew and she headed straight for it. When the waitress, a girl in her late teens, came to her table she ordered an Americano coffee and added, "Hey Julie, seems to have been a terrible tragedy around the corner in Mr Newman's house. Did you hear anything about it?"

"Can't say that I did but you know what Mr Fancy Newman is like?" said the girl.

"In what way?" asked Shirley.

"Well, apparently he had split up with his wife before he moved into Elm Grove and a classmate of mine used to babysit his daughter Tracey. And believe me, she had many a story to tell. He seemed to like them young. If you know what I mean."

Just then her cell phone rang. "What is it Bo?" she said.

"Get over here fast Shirley, there are lots of people coming and going here."

"Sorry, but I have to go." she said to Julie, handing her a generous tip. "I will get the coffee later."

As she arrived back at the barrier she could see that another ambulance had arrived and also at least three large black cars. "Any idea who's who in there now, Bo?"

"The first car to arrive was the Chief of Police, Ned Brennan. In the second car I recognized Jeff Suarez, Gregg Newman's Election Manager and two senior Party members. Just can't remember their names. They went straight in to the house and haven't come out since. Then a very upset looking, middle aged woman, went in and seconds later I heard a scream. She has just been escorted out in an obviously distraught state. That is her sitting on the seat outside the house being comforted by a female police officer. I heard one of the spectators say that she looked like a Mrs Lummox, whose daughter Angie used to babysit the Newman's daughter Tracey. But that is just hearsay at this point in time." said Bo.

"Keep filming Bo, I will be back in a second." said Shirley as she raced back to the coffee shop.

As she got to the shop, Julie was just finished serving a customer but stopped when she saw Shirley waving a ten-dollar bill in her hand. "Julie, can you do me a big favor please? Just come with me to the barrier and tell me if you know the name of a woman sitting outside Gregg Newman's house."

With a quick glance to make sure she wasn't seen, Julie raced off ahead of Shirley. "Oh my God! That's Angie Lummox's mother. What is she doing there?"

"Thanks Julie, that's all I wanted to know. You wouldn't happen to know her address by any chance, would you?"

"Yep, they live just a few doors down from me at number sixteen, Beach Lawn." replied Julie.

"You had better get back to work Julie and I will be back for the coffee soon," said Shirley.

"Hold it!" said Bo. "There is something happening. Looks like Gregg Newman is being brought out to the ambulance in a wheelchair. Yes, that's him and that is Al

McNally, his attorney with him. Both have now entered the ambulance and it is heading off. If only we had someone to follow it to see where it was going to."

Chapter 4

Leaving Bo and the rest of the team in position Shirley headed to a quiet spot to report to her boss. "Hi Butch, things are hotting up here. Gregg Newman, together with Al McNally, left in an ambulance. Newman was brought out in a wheelchair but was able, with help, to climb into the ambulance. Unfortunately, we have no one to follow it to see where it goes. Gregg Newman's Election Manager and two of the election team have also arrived and are ensconced in the house ever since. Finally, a very distraught woman arrived and was brought in to the house from where Bo heard her scream. She is now being comforted outside the house by a female police officer. I have been told that she is a Mrs Lummox whose daughter used to babysit the Newman's daughter, Tracey. I also have been told that the same Mr Newman has quite a reputation regarding young girls."

"Well done Shirley!" said Butch "However we must be ultra-careful with this one. We must stick rigidly to the absolute facts as we are dealing with very powerful people here. We have just announced our exclusive on the nine o'clock news, sticking to the police announcement and giving a short clip of your report. Now on the ten o'clock bulletin we will again repeat the exclusive and then Norman will go to you to cover the location etc. and then show a few clips of the activity around the house. By then we should be ready for the police statement. Under no circumstances can we speculate on anything. OK?"

"That gives us approximately forty-five minutes before the announcement. I am going to get myself a coffee and some more information." said Shirley, as she headed back to the coffee shop. "Check with the others and let me know what they want and I will have it sent over to them."

By the time she got there, she found that Julie had finished her shift and had left. The new waitress was a more mature woman who had no opinion and was not in the mood for gossip, so Shirley just sipped her coffee and thought about the opportunity she had just been given to prove herself. What would the more senior reporters do in a case like this? If they had uncovered the story would they be prepared to just sit back and let Butch dictate the announcement or would they demand that they would have a say in what went out on air? Then would they start to do some further investigation off their own bat? It was at a time like this that she was sorry not to have a partner she could confide in. Certainly not Jeff and his fishing buddies.

By the time she got back to the barrier she had to beat her way in to Bo. As predicted, at least thirty reporters and cameramen were jostling for prime position, but Bo and his crew were not going to be pushed around. This was their gig.

Exactly on the stroke of ten o'clock, and just as Norman led the ten o'clock bulletin with the breaking news 'Tragedy at Elm Grove', he immediately cued Shirley in live from the scene. Just as Police Chief, Ned Brennan, approached the barrier and read a brief statement;

"At approximately seven thirty this evening a neighbor who had been babysitting Mr Newman's daughter became alarmed when Mr Newman did not come to collect his daughter. When he failed to make contact with him, he entered Mr Gregg Newman's home through the open front door.

Once inside he found the body of a young girl and Mr Newman in an unconscious condition. He immediately called the emergency number.

At this early point in our investigation, we are not in a position to speculate as to the sequence of events in this tragic incident but will keep you posted as to our findings. We wish to send our condolences to the family of the deceased young girl and will not be releasing her name until her extended family are notified. Thank you for your cooperation."

With that he turned and, ignoring the babble of questions hurled at him, headed back to the house.

"Thank you Shirley. Can you tell us what has been happening since you broke the story?" intoned Norman in her earpiece. Oh my God, he is asking me, thought Shirley. Norman is asking me!

Pulling herself together she broke into the usual patter. "Well Norman as you can see the activity around here is intense. We have had a number of ambulances at the scene and just about fifteen minutes ago we saw Mr Newman being wheeled out in a wheelchair and entering one of the ambulances, with his attorney, Mr Al McNally."

"Was he unable to walk? Did he have to be helped into the ambulance?" asked Norman.

"As soon as he got to the ambulance he got out of the chair and stepped into the ambulance." said Shirley.

"Thanks Shirley, and yes, we do have a shot of that." said Norman as the playback showed Mr Newman emerging from the house and getting into the ambulance.

"We also had the arrival of the Chief of Police and Mr Jeff Suarez, Mr Newman's Election Manager and some senior Party officials some time ago. You can see the big black cars outside the house. Hold on there while we get a close up of the front of the house." With that the camera zoomed in on each car and anyone in the vicinity of the front door.

"Thank you, Shirley, for bringing that story to us. No doubt we will be hearing a lot more of it in the coming days."

"Thanks Norman. From me, Shirley Green, news reporter at NTTV, good night and keep watching NTTV."

"And now back to the rest of the news." said Norman. "At approximately six fifteen p.m. a car emerging from one of the steep slip roads near Junction 14, apparently ran out of control and jumped the guard rails and careered onto the freeway where it was hit by a sixteen-wheeler which then jack-knifed, hitting a number of cars. Latest reports say that three people are dead and at least twenty injured. Here is a report from our reporter, Tom Waite, who was at the scene…"

Chapter 5

As soon as Al McNally had Gregg Newman safely signed in to a private room, and given strict instructions to the doctor in charge that he was not to be allowed any visitors, he gave him instructions as to what checks he wanted carried out on Gregg. His next move was to call Judge Leo Forrest who was the local Party Chairman. "Hi, Leo, he has done it again and this time I don't think we can bail him out."

"What and who are you talking about Al? For God's sake calm down."

Ten minutes later, when Al had filled him in on the events, it was Leo who needed calming down. "For Christ's sake! What got into him? I thought he had learned to keep his trousers on after the last time, four years ago. I had better call an emergency meeting of the Election Committee immediately."

"Gentlemen, we have a problem," began Leo, two hours later, as he faced the ten men seated around the boardroom table. "A very serious problem has arisen. Al has just filled me in on the events that have happened in Gregg Newman's house. I suggest that Al takes over from here and gives you the facts as we now know them."

"Thanks, Leo," began Al, "I was called to Gregg Newman's house this evening by a neighbor of his and found the police there. They had been called to investigate the death of a young girl in the house. She had been tied to the bed and strangled by a belt. They found Gregg, who appeared to be either drunk or drugged, in a state of undress. I managed to keep him quiet and have had him admitted to Calvary Hospital to have him examined. I might add that he kept muttering about an intruder and his wife's perfume. None of which made any sense."

"Was there any one else in the house?" asked Teddy Moran, chairman of the local bank.

"No, and the police are not looking for anyone else, either. They appear to have an open and shut case against Gregg."

"An open and shut case of what exactly?" asked Mark Reilly, Gregg's boss at the law firm.

"Well, it looks like a sex game that went wrong but whatever, he could be charged with either murder or accidental homicide. In the meantime, I have managed to keep Gregg away from the police on the basis that he is not in a fit condition to be questioned. However, I can't hold them back from him for much longer as the media have got hold of part of the story. Now we have to decide our move. We have less than three weeks to the election. Do we brazen it out and hope for the best or do we cut our losses and run? Gentlemen, that is the question we have to decide on."

"OK, hold your horses a minute," said Judge Forrest. "Before we can make any decision we have to know the full facts. Is this an unfortunate domestic accident that can be explained away? Or is it more sinister than that? Is this an expose into the darker side of our potential mayor?"

"Well," said Teddy Moran, "we know what Gregg's history is like, don't we? It was never good, was it? We knew what he was like but this time we have a dead girl in his house. This is a completely new ball game. He has to go."

"More than three years ago I strongly recommended that we cut him loose but I was overruled, wasn't I?" said Mark.

"Hindsight is a perfect science, isn't it?" said Al Mc Nally drily. "That time we all believed it was just his wife was the problem, didn't we? So we had her declared insane and had her put far away from here. Now Gregg is talking about an intruder in the house using her perfume. What do you make of that?"

"How the hell could she have been there for Christ's sake? She's locked up, isn't she?" said Jeff Suarez, Gregg's Election Manager.

"Obviously he must have been high on something or other at the time?" suggested Leo. "Whatever the case it was, we need to act and act fast. However, I believe that just because he has trouble keeping his trousers on, doesn't take from his candidacy for mayor. Look at the past number of presidents who had the same problem?" said Al.

"Look, Al, it isn't just a question of having sex." said Teddy. "After all he is a single adult, so that isn't the problem. For Christ's sake, there is a dead girl this time. The problem for him and for the Party, is his attraction to young girls. And now the probability that he will be charged with a sexual offence. It is also a question of the possibility of the case against his wife being reopened by the nosey press. You know what they are like if they get a sniff of something irregular? I think the risk is too great. We should consider pulling him out and substituting some other hopeful."

"Ok, here is what we will do." said Leo. "Al, you talk to Gregg and then set up a meeting with Chief Brennan and see in what direction he is leaning. Teddy, you draft a possible press release to cover the crisis, claim mental problems due to pressure of work or something like that. The rest of you draw up a short list of possible substitutes. We will meet again tomorrow at 11.00am here in my office."

Chapter 6

Eight a.m. on Saturday morning in the incident room that had been set up in Police HQ and the mood was one of 'let's get this over with', as an obviously stressed Chief Ned Brennan faced the team. "OK, Eddie, what have we got?"

Carefully reading his notes Eddie began his report. "On being called to the home of Mr Gregg Newman at approximately 7:30p.m. yesterday evening, we found a young girl tied to a bed and strangled by a belt which appeared to belong to Mr Newman. His, and only his, fingerprints were on the belt. Mr Newman had been removed from the room where he had been found sitting on the floor beside the bed. He appeared to be in what looked like a drunken stupor. Apart from requesting that his attorney be contacted, the only thing he muttered was to say that an intruder had been there."

"On examining the room, we found Mr Newman's clothing neatly folded on the chair by the bed and we located, on top of the wardrobe, a micro security camera which was sensor activated and also set on a timer. We have not as yet got the results from the lab. When his attorney arrived he advised him to say nothing." He said.

"He said his wife was there. Was she?" asked the Chief.

"No, not exactly," Eddie replied. "Newman said that there was an intruder there and that there was a scent of the perfume his wife used, all very vague and confused. He was also muttering something about his Taser gun. We checked the building thoroughly and there was no indication that there was anyone else there. On checking for finger prints, the only ones we found belonged to Mr Newman, the deceased girl, and Mr Spinks, his neighbor who had been babysitting Mr Newman's daughter and who called in the situation. We also found a pay-as-you-go cell phone in Mr Newman's bedside locker. On examining it we found a text message to the deceased asking her to meet him at his house that evening as usual. Mr Newman's prints were on the cell phone."

"So, on the face of that it looks like an open and shut case?" said the Chief. "The only question therefore is whether the charge should be murder one or accidental homicide?"

"Before we go that far," said Lennie Bareman from forensics. "Remember who we are dealing with here. We will need to tread cautiously. Firstly, we need to have a full toxicology on Mr Newman to establish what exactly he was on. That will take at least forty-eight hours from the time we have him tested."

"More importantly we need to interview Mr Newman," said Eddie.

"I'll have a chat with the DA and advise Al McNally that the sooner he gives us access to his client the better. Otherwise we will just have to charge him. We certainly appear to have an absolute case against him. In the meantime, Eddie and Maria had better check up on the whereabouts of Mrs Newman."

Looking around the room at the team, Eddie asked if anyone had information on her.

"Your best bet is to Google her," said Walt Carter, one of the oldest in the team. "I do however remember some years back seeing photographs of both of them in the press, at various functions. She was a strikingly beautiful looking woman. However, she suddenly seemed to just disappear from his side. Then whenever he appeared in the press, which was very often, now that he had a high profile with the Party more often than not he was seen socializing with various beautiful women."

"If they are divorced there will have to be a paper trail. Maria, will you follow up on that and also see if you can talk to Mr Spinks. He should be able to give us the lowdown on the family history." said the Chief. "And check out the neighbors again. Someone must have either seen or heard something."

Chapter 7

"Well done to all of you and particularly to Shirley who was sharp enough to spot what was going down." said Butch Collins, at the morning team briefing meeting, "Not only were we the first to break the news on our nine o'clock news, but our coverage on the ten o' clock news was way ahead of the other stations. Interestingly enough the newspapers have just one small mention of the 'incident' on page five. Someone is keeping this very tight."

"I would also like to add my congratulations to Shirley for the professional way she slotted in to her first live broadcast." said Norman Wilder. "No one would guess that it was her first broadcast."

Shirley blushed and pretended to be engrossed in her notebook. But her smile said everything.

"Ok, so where do we go from here?" said Butch. "We still don't have a detailed statement from the police as to what exactly happened. They are really keeping this one tight."

Turning to Alan Brody who was one of the longest serving reporters at the station he said, "You get down to the police station and see if you can get an interview with Eddie McGrane. You are an old drinking buddy of his – aren't you?" Then turning to Shirley, "Your job will be to look into the human interest side of the story. Check out the family, his wife, his neighbors and particularly the babysitters. We need to keep ahead of the opposition on this."

As Shirley picked up her notebook and recorder and headed for the door she felt that all her Christmases had come together. She was being given a challenging job at last. And Butch had actually complimented her. What a difference a day makes, she mused, as she made her first call which was to the coffee shop off Elm Grove, to see if the waitress Julie was on duty.

Julie seemed to have a lot of local knowledge, if only she would part with it. Shirley felt that she already had gained her confidence. As luck would have it, she was on duty and remembering the very generous tip Shirley had given her the previous evening, she readily agreed to meet up with her when she finished her shift.

"What's going on?" asked Julie, as they were seated in the local bar.

"We are not sure," replied Shirley, "but it appears that something serious happened at Gregg Newman's house. We are trying to get any kind of information that might help the police. Can you tell me anything about Mrs Newman?"

"Not really," replied Julie. "When they came to live here about four years ago there were only Mr Newman and Tracey. Since then he had built up a reputation as a 'ladies man' with a particular liking for young women. Some of the stories the girls who had been babysitting whispered about to their friends in school, were mind-blowing. Of course he was also known for his generous payments to special babysitters. That was why rumours emerged."

"Did Angie ever talk about Tracey's mother?"

"Not really except for one time when I was telling her that my mother was in hospital. She did say something about Tracey saying that that was where all mothers end up."

"You mentioned something about Angie's diary." said Shirley. "Can you tell me more about that?"

"Well, one day Angie was sporting a very chic designer outfit and I asked her where she got it. She was all excited and began saying that Mr Newman had given it to her, for services rendered, as she put it. Then she said, of course I am no fool, all services are recorded in my diary and only I know where that is. Someday I will give you a peep at it – when you are old enough!"

Having thanked Julie for her information and given her another generous tip, Shirley decided to trace Gregg Newman's movements and hopefully that would lead her to Mrs Newman. But where to look? Of course it was obvious, wasn't it? Just ask the police, they should know.

So she decided to go home and put on her best outfit, actually it was her only good one, before heading for the police station.

She nearly lost her nerve as she approached the building which was located in a side street off of Columbus Avenue. The building itself looked as if it hadn't been painted since the time of Columbus. Paint was flaking from every window frame and the front door looked as if it had been the object of every known missile that could have been thrown at it over many a year. Outside, the street had the appearance of a wrecker's yard with cars of all shapes and sizes parked in no particular order.

"Can I see Detective Eddie McGrane?" she asked the policeman behind the desk, when she eventually entered the building.

"Have you an appointment?" he replied, in a tone that seemed to say, 'I know damn well you don't'.

"No, I don't but I think I have information that he will be glad to get," Shirley replied, in her best sophisticated voice.

"What's the name Miss?" he replied, without looking at her.

Ten minutes later Eddie arrived at the desk. "Ok Miss Green, what do you have for me?"

The first thing that Shirley noticed about him was his easy manner. There was none of the macho behaviour usually attached to people in uniform. Then again Eddie didn't wear a uniform. He was a detective. Maybe it was the way he looked at her, she wasn't sure, but something passed between them. Something telepathic.

"Well, as you probably know, I work for NTTV. I spoke to you outside Mr Newman's house. We have been following the events that took place at Newman's house from a number of angles. I think we might be able to help each other from time to time, don't you? For example, I am following up the family angle and I would like to find out something about Mrs Newman. Who is she? Is she still alive, and if so where is she? Things like that." said Shirley.

"And what, if anything can you tell me?" replied Eddie.

"I happen to know that Angie, the babysitter, kept a diary." replied Shirley.

"Wow. How do you know that?" replied Eddie.

"Fair exchange is no robbery, as the saying goes. Your turn to give me a lead now."

"Well, I'm not giving away any secrets. Up to three or four years ago, from what I am told, the Newman's lived over in Oldtown where both worked in a small local law firm. Mark Reilly, a partner in one of the biggest law firms in the city, apparently saw him as an up and coming lawyer, and more importantly, as an asset for the Democratic Party and possible candidate for future political success. He made him an offer he couldn't refuse, so he moved up here to the city. Mrs Newman didn't move with him. Why I don't know. Now tell me about the diary." said Eddie.

Having told Eddie exactly what Julie had told her she decided to follow up on what Eddie had told her and drive to Oldtown, which was less than two hour's drive, south of the city on the tip of the lower lake.

Less than two hours later she saw the sign for the turnoff for Oldtown.

Welcome to Oldtown, population 25250.

As she drove into the town she felt as if she had been transported back to the 1950's. The Barbeque Joint shared a building with a gas station and the Pizza Diner shared a building with an antique store. In the town square the monument to the many sons and daughters of Oldtown, who had lost their lives in World War Two, stood forlornly beneath well-weathered Stars and Stripes.

What was once a very quaint and colorful town now looked as if the entire town needed to be painted.

Her first stop, when she arrived there, was at the local library where she requested copies of the local newspaper, going back five years. Two hours later she found it, exactly what she was looking for, a photo of Gregg Newman and his wife Alice at the local New Year's Ball. Her first thought was of how dashing they both looked, that was four years ago.

Next she headed for the town hall to check on the register of deaths and divorces. She found nothing under deaths but eventually found the record of the divorce, three years ago. She now needed to get the record of the details of the divorce. She was stuck. She needed help.

"Hi Butch, do you by any chance know anyone at the Oldtown Chronicle?" said Shirley as she was put through to her boss.

"And where might you be Shirley? I thought you were working on the Gregg Newman case?" replied Butch. "Remember me? I'm your boss!"

"Sorry about that," said Shirley, "I am trying to trace Gregg Newman's wife and the trail has brought me to Oldtown and I am now stuck. I need a contact here that might open another door for me."

"As a matter of fact I do know someone. Don Harding is the editor and a classmate of mine. I will call him and tell him to expect you. And don't forget to keep me in the loop!" said Butch.

Chapter 8

As Eddie was heading back to his desk, having got off the phone to Shirley, his Chief spotted him and called him over.

"Hi Eddie, any developments in the Newman case?" he asked. "City Hall are pressing hard on this one. There is a lot at stake and big names are asking if we really have a case or not."

"I have spoken to Al and he is willing to share the toxicology report he has requested from the hospital. He expects to have it in the morning. That will save us some time." replied Eddie.

"Yes, that's all good and fine, but can we interview Newman? That's the sixty-four-thousand-dollar question." replied the Chief. "We really need to get immediate access to him. Time is of the essence now."

"Once we get the report we will then be in a position to judge whether the possible charge should be murder one or accidental homicide. But in my opinion, it is one or the other. If it was anyone other than Gregg Newman, we wouldn't be even having this conversation." said Eddie.

"Just make sure there are no loopholes and double-check every procedure at least twice. We can't afford to make a mistake and find Newman elected as our new mayor and boss!" said the Chief.

"Oh, by the way, I got information about Gregg Newman's apparent attraction to 'young women'." said Eddie, making quotation signs with his fingers. "Especially those who babysat for him. It appears that the deceased had kept a diary of sorts in which she kept records of her encounters with Newman. Maria and I are calling to Angie's mother to see if we can get confirmation on this."

"And where, may I ask, did this piece of information come from?" demanded the Chief.

"A reporter from NTTV called to the station and volunteered it to us."

"Did he now? And I don't suppose he wanted any inside information in return. Did he?"

"Well, in the first instance, it was a woman who called, not a man. And yes she was looking for information on the whereabouts of Mrs Newman. As you know, we have no idea where she is. However, we now know that a diary exists which may help our case."

"Ok, just as long as you keep your distance from any of the media – no buddy buddy."

Having collected Maria, they headed off to interview Julie, just to confirm Shirley's information at first hand.

However, they discovered that Julie wasn't too keen to talk to the police about anything, especially about something as serious as the death of a young girl who was known to her. When they brought up the question of the diary, she became nervous and anxious so they decided to back off for now.

Leaving Julie, Eddie told Maria that they were now going to Angie's house to try and locate her hidden diary. Maria suggested that perhaps this wasn't an appropriate time to make such a call as her parents were in deep shock and they had already been interviewed the previous day. Now they were going to be asked to search for a hidden diary, looking through the private side of Angie's life. Not a good move. As a compromise, Eddie suggested they call just to see how the funeral arrangements were coming on and then, if the occasion arose, they could raise the question of the diary.

When they got to the house they found it full of people, with neighbors and friends coming and going. Having expressed their condolences to Angie's parents and again confirming that they could not say when Angie's body would be released for burial, Eddie asked when it would be suitable for him and his partner to come and talk to them in private. They also mentioned that they would like to have a look at Angie's room where they said they might find something that would help them to understand what had happened to her. Hesitantly they agreed that the following morning at eleven a.m. would be the best time as at that time the chances of neighbors calling would be slim.

As they got back into the car, Eddie said, "Maria, you being a woman, where do you think a sixteen-year-old would hide an intimate diary? One that she sure as hell wouldn't want her parents to ever find."

"Well, let's work it out. She wouldn't have it in her school bag, too risky taking it to school. Not in her clothes drawers, her mother would have free access to those." said Maria.

"How about under her mattress?" suggested Eddie.

"No, for something as important as this, it would be too obvious." replied Maria. "Her mother is small so I would think it would be somewhere up high where her mother would be unlikely to get to."

"Ok, that sounds very reasonable, when we get there tomorrow, you keep her parents talking and I will ask to have a quick look at her room. If your intuition is right, I should very quickly be able to check any high places there might be."

When they got back to the station Eddie decided

to call a mini-meeting to go over all of the facts, as they had them and make sure they had covered all of the bases. Luckily, just as they arrived they met Lennie from forensics. He was about to go on a call but agreed to attend the meeting, provided it would be a very short one. Officer Andy Maguire and Walt Carter were available. Of course they still didn't have the toxicology or medical reports and also, and most importantly, they hadn't interviewed Gregg Newman either.

"As we are all very much aware, this is a highly sensitive case and the Chief wants to be sure we have every detail covered before we make an arrest. So let's go over exactly what we have in a critical manner."

"Walt, I want you to just listen and identify any weak spots. Andy, you start from the time you got the call to go to 45 Elm Grove."

"We were patrolling in the area, Officer Walt Carter and I, when dispatch requested us to attend at the address as there had been an incident there. We were not to use sirens or flashing lights. When we arrived we were let into the house by Arthur Spinks, the man who had called in the incident."

"Ok Walt, hold it there. Close your eyes and just recall your first impression as you got to the house."

"I suppose my first impression was that it was a very

secluded and badly lit place. Lots of hedges and trees and street lights were imitation gaslights. If you know what I mean." replied Walt.

"Very good, but at what stage did the security lights come on?" said Eddie.

"Wait a while, I don't recall any security lights coming on at number 45. Later on, when the TV crew arrived, I recall security lights coming on where they were parked outside of the cordon. But now that you mention it, there were no lights outside of Gregg Newman's house." said Walt.

Taking a marker, Eddie put a note on the whiteboard, 'check security lighting and cctv cameras in the area.'

"So, what happened next?" asked Eddie.

"A Mr Arthur Spinks met us at the front door and let us in." said Walt.

"Ok. Now, close your eyes again, and recall what your first impressions were." said Eddie.

"My first impression was of a very distraught man, who introduced himself to us as Mr Arthur Spinks, standing in a dimly lit hallway, who stumbled over something as we came in. We later discovered that it was a briefcase that was lying on the ground. I was also aware of a strong smell of whiskey in the house and something else. Yes, a strong smell of perfume as we entered the bedroom. Again, this room was dimly lit but I could see someone lying on the bed and a man sitting on the floor beside the bed. He was clothed only in his underpants. Beside him was an almost empty bottle of Johnny Walker. The man kept muttering something about an intruder being in the house. He was almost incoherent."

"Ok," said Eddie as he went back to the whiteboard. "We have five questions. One, any evidence of an intruder being in the house? Two, how did Mr Spinks get into the house? Three, who turned off the camera? Four, how much whiskey, if any, did Gregg Newman drink? Five, where did the smell of perfume come from? Are we missing anything Walt?"

"Have we examined the record of the alarm company to see when the alarm was deactivated? Was it on when Angie arrived? That whole area needs to be thoroughly examined. Secondly, the business of the CCTV cameras malfunctioning needs to be examined further. It seems an unlikely coincidence that the cameras went on the blink that week and that as soon as they were fixed they went off again and again." replied Walt.

"Ok, let's get to work. Walt, you take the alarm and CCTV issues and see what you find. Maria and I have an appointment with Angie's parents' tomorrow and we will see what the normal procedure was when she was asked to babysit. In the meantime, we will re-interview Mr Spinks."

"Lennie, I want you to comb the building, front and back, for any trace of an intruder being there. If this is going to be Gregg Newman's defense, we must be absolutely certain that we have checked and re-checked all possibilities. And don't forget to check on the perfume." said Eddie.

Chapter 9

On their way to visit Mr Spinks, Eddie said, "I'd like to have another chat with Julie. I have a feeling that she could tell us a lot more of what was going on between Gregg Newman and Angie. What do you think?"

"I think she doesn't like talking to cops full stop." replied Maria. "Also it is difficult to differentiate between gossip, jealousy and fact, when it comes to talking to teenagers."

"Very true, but maybe she would open up again to that TV girl if she were to approach her." said Eddie.

"Oh, you mean Shirley, the one you keep talking about? The one you think is hot? Would that be the TV girl you are talking about? I can sense the chemistry between you two every time you mention her name." replied Maria.

"Well, when you put it like that… Yes, that's the one who just might get through to Julie," said Eddie, ignoring the jibe.

As they pulled into Elm Grove, they noticed that the scene was still cordoned off and an officer stood outside the door. "How long have you been here on duty?" asked Eddie.

"I came on duty at one p.m. sir." replied the officer.

"Tell me, have you noticed any of the security lighting coming on since you arrived here?"

"No sir, I was actually conscious of how dim the lighting was in this whole area as the evening drew in."

"Thanks, officer. We are just calling to number 35, around the corner to the man who called in the incident."

"Let's hope Mr Spinks doesn't go out on a Saturday evening." said Eddie as they approached number 35.

As they waited for someone to answer the door, they were aware that the security lighting came on for not only number 35 but for number 33 as well.

"It looks like the security lighting problem is confined to the houses around the corner only." remarked Maria.

"Yes. Interesting. We had better get someone on that first thing on Monday morning. They would hardly be working on a Sunday." said Eddie.

"Good evening officers." said Mr Spinks as he opened the door. "I see you don't take the weekend off."

"Well, we hope to take tomorrow off, Mr Spinks, but right now we need to keep moving while people's memories are not distorted by what they will read on the Sunday newspapers," replied Eddie.

"Come on in, and most people call me Art. Now tell

me what more I can do for you. This is a dreadful tragedy."

"The first thing we would like to know is who is minding Tracey? She must be shattered by the events that have happened."

"Tracey has been staying with us up to now but Mr Newman's attorney has been on the phone to say that he is on his way to pick her up. Apparently, he has made arrangements for Mr Newman, who is still under doctor's care, and Tracey to book into a hotel until this mess is sorted out."

"That makes a lot of sense. Now what we would like you to do is to tell us what you know of Mr Newman. What you know of his background, his family, his habits, and anything that comes to mind. No matter how unimportant it may seem to you. I know that is a tall order, especially on a Saturday evening."

"Where to start?" said Art, "Well, when he moved in here about three years ago with his five-year-old daughter Tracey. We hit it off straight away, possibly because Tracey was around our Jenny's age and was an ideal pal for her. Also Gregg had been enrolled as a member of the Country Club and was a mean golfer, so I had a very convenient golf partner."

"So what about Mrs Newman?"

"I got the impression, and it is only an impression,

mind you, that he was recently divorced. Any time I brought the subject up he was very short with his answers. I supposed it was still very raw in his mind. I do recall hearing Tracey mention to Jenny that her Mom had been sick. However, that was just kid's talk." said Art.

"Ok, tell me about the babysitting arrangements over the years," asked Eddie.

"As you know, Gregg is a very busy man and was from day one. It's not easy, especially for a man, to bring up a child on his own. As a result, he would draw on my wife, Lucy and me when possible and on local babysitters in general."

"And were there a particular number of local sitters that you know of?"

"Well, apart from poor Angie, she used to sit for us also – a lovely girl, God bless her – there were at least two others that I recall. You see if Gregg got one that was satisfactory, he would tell us and vice versa. Hold on and I will get my phone book. I'm sure the numbers are still in it." said Art.

"I wonder if there is a pattern here." said Maria, as they waited for Art to return.

"Yes, here we are," said Art, as he returned with his phone book. "First there was Suzanne and she was followed by Nora and then by Amanda. We often wondered why they gave up babysitting as they were all very good and seemed to be happy with our arrangements. Anyway, Gregg always managed to find another one."

"Did you or your wife ever ask them why they were giving up the babysitting?" asked Eddie.

"Well, Lucy always looked after these kinds of arrangements. I understood that, while it would have been inconvenient at the time, their explanations, such as interfering with their study, were understandable." replied Art.

"Ok, can you let us have their full names and addresses and contact numbers, please." asked Maria.

"Looking back again at the events of last Friday evening, if you don't mind." said Eddie. "What exactly were the arrangements you had with Gregg Newman?"

"Lucy was taking Jennie to the mall when she collected her from school and had arranged to take Tracey with her. She had cleared all of this with Gregg who said he would collect her from our house at about seven thirty. He was aware that we had a prior arrangement and would be leaving the house by eight p.m. at the latest." replied Art.

"So, at what stage did you try to contact Gregg?"

"Normally he was very punctual. So, when he didn't arrive, or call, by seven forty p.m., I rang his cell phone and was put on to his answer message. By seven fifty, having called a number of times, I walked around to his house, which is just around the corner. His car was in the driveway. When I got to the front door I was surprised to find it open." said Art.

"When you say it was open, what exactly do you mean?"

"Well it was probably just two or three inches open, I suppose," replied Art.

"Did you go inside immediately?"

"No, I rang the bell a number of times and called through the door, but got no reply. I then pushed in the door and went inside, calling Gregg as I went from room to room. It was then I found him in the bedroom, sitting on the floor beside the bed. It was awful. He was completely disorientated from what I could tell."

"Did you talk to him or touch anything?"

"I asked him if he was alright and then I saw the girl tied to the bed and she wasn't moving. I didn't know what to do. I suppose, by instinct I called the emergency number and that triggered the arrival of the paramedics and your officers." said Art.

"So, at what stage did you call his attorney?"

"Your officer began to ask him questions, as he appeared to begin to focus on what was going on. At that stage he called out to me from the room to get in contact with Al McNally urgently. I know Mr McNally from the club." said Art.

"Did you get a feeling that there was someone else in the house or had been in the house?"

"I don't think so. The house is always so clean and somewhat clinical but this time there was a strong smell of whiskey, and funnily enough, some kind of perfume."

"Look, sorry for messing up your Saturday evening, and we do appreciate your help. One final question, is it possible that someone could get in through the back of the house?"

"Possible? I think everything is possible but as you will see, all of these houses back on to a laneway and are protected by a very high wall with razor wire on top of it. Each house has a small gateway into the garden for garbage access but each door is treble locked and connected to the alarm system. So, is it possible? Yes. But in my opinion, not really." replied Art.

"Talking about the alarm, have you had any problems with your alarm recently?" asked Eddie.

"No, I can't say that we have, but just let me ask Lucy. She is here more often than I am during the daytime."

"Hi honey," said Art, as soon as Lucy came into the room. "Do you recall us having any problems with our alarm system over the past few months. It appears that Gregg did have problems with his system."

"No, I can't recall any such occasion." said Lucy. "However, from time to time I would be aware of Gregg's going off briefly, just before it would be turned off. I never thought much of it."

"Did this happen very often?" asked Eddie.

"I think it would generally be around Friday lunchtime, that would always be the day I would have the girls over for an early snack lunch in the conservatory. Sometimes I would notice Gregg pass by the window, on his lunchtime jog." said Lucy.

"Thank you both for seeing us at such short notice. Apologies again for intruding on your Saturday." said Eddie, as he and Maria got up to leave.

As they climbed back into the car, Eddie said,

"I think it is time to call it a day. Go home to your husband and kid and try and salvage the rest of the weekend. I'm going to grab a burger and watch the ball game. See you on Monday. Hopefully the rest of the team will have uncovered some more of the detail."

Chapter 10

That evening, as he watched the ball game, his mind kept going over the case and each time it came back to the babysitters. When it did, that brought him back to Shirley, the TV girl. Eventually he decided to call her on the pretext of making an appointment to see her at the station on Monday.

"Hi there, this is Detective Eddie McGrane calling, and sorry for interrupting your Saturday evening. You may remember we spoke briefly yesterday regarding the waitress in the coffee shop?"

"Oh yes, I do. Did you have any luck with her?" replied Shirley.

"Well, that is why I am calling you. I think she is more comfortable talking to you than to me. I got a very short response. I was wondering if you would be free on Monday to have a chat with me?"

"Unfortunately, I will be out of town so it will have to be Tuesday or Wednesday."

"Oh! Look this is very important. Any chance we could meet this evening at the coffee shop? For a coffee? I really would appreciate it if you could."

"OK, give me an hour to put on my public face and

I will see you there." Shirley wasn't going anywhere and hadn't heard from 'boyfriend' Jeff since he headed off for the weekend with his friends. And Eddie was easy on the eyes, if somewhat too focused on his work. Also, he was probably married with a clutch of kids at home, but then if he had, why was he ringing her on a Saturday evening? She asked herself.

"Hi, thanks for coming," Eddie said as he rose to shake hands with her, as she entered the coffee shop. "Again, sorry for messing up your evening."

"Not to worry. I was just in the middle of a very hot date," said Shirley. "But one must serve one's country and all that kind of crap. I'll have a cappuccino, if you are asking?"

Shirley looked around and saw Julie working up at the other end of the café,

"You must be having a really good day." said Eddie, "Or are you always this cheerful?"

"Oh, you should see me on a good day. I'm really something. Now tell me detective, what can I do for you?"

"Well, as I said on the phone, I had a chat with Julie and I must have hit a nerve with her or else I am losing my charm. I got zilch out of her. So, I am wondering if seeing you here with me, she might be more receptive to telling me more about her buddies from class and their babysitting experiences."

"And if she does, what do I get in return?"

"Aren't you getting a cappuccino?"

"You must be joking, detective. I could have had that in my apartment."

"All alone in an apartment on a Saturday evening? Surely this is better than that?"

"Look who's talking? – have you no home to go to?"

"Ok, here's the deal. Let's see if we can get Julie to talk to me. If she does I'll treat you to dinner, a small one. I know a little Italian restaurant, Mario's Place, on Shore road, you might know it? How does that sound?"

"Oh yes, I know it. Isn't that the one with the decking built on stilts over the lake? By the way, are you asking me out for a date, detective?" said Shirley

"Yeah, it's a nice place to sit out and to eat when the sun is shining but not at this time of year – unless you particularly like the cold! And no, I'm not asking you to marry me, it's just a dinner. Of course if you have something better to do, I fully understand."

"Well, when you put it like that, I suppose I could do worse."

"Well, now that that has been sorted, can you have a word in Julie's ear and let me get on with my investigation, please?"

Five minutes later Shirley returned to the table having

spoken to Julie.

"She says she will call to the station on Monday morning, before her shift which starts at noon, and will talk to you."

"Well done, that sounds great. Now let's head for Mario's and I hope you like Italian cuisine."

When they arrive at Mario's they were surprised to find the place buzzing and found difficulty in getting a place to park. Inside, every table seemed to be occupied. At Eddie's favorite table in the corner sat a Stephen King look-a-like, reading a book and picking his nose. Oblivious to the world around him and to Eddie's stare! In the background, Dean Martin was gently crooning Volare.

"Hi Eddie, good to see you. You were missed at practice on Saturday. Joey said that you were tied up in some murder case or something like that." said the head waiter, as he came over to greet them.

"Yeah, Giovani, some of us have to work you know!"

"Is this what you call work," replied Giovani, as he eyed Shirley, "Just remember we have the semi-final on Saturday next. Hope you can get to practice on Wednesday. The kids need you. Hold on here while I find a table for you."

As Giovani went in search of an empty table or even a

space to put another table, Shirley said, "What's this about practice and semi-finals?"

"Ah, nothing. I just give a hand with the junior football team from time to time."

"So are you some kind of coach?"

"Well, I used to play a bit but unfortunately I did in my knee two years ago so now I am reduced to watching others play. That's all."

Just them, Giovani beckoned them over to a table that had just seemed to appear out of nowhere.

Chapter 11

Monday mornings in the station were always slow burners. However, today, by nine thirty the full team was present in the incident room.

Copies of the Sunday newspapers were scattered around the conference table with banner headlines, such as, 'What went on in number 45 Elm Grove? Was it a sex party that went wrong?', 'Young girl found dead in home of election candidate.' However, the broadsheet presses still seemed to be underplaying the events.

As they waited for the Chief to arrive, Maria asked Eddie if he had contacted his 'TV girl'?

"As a matter of fact I did and as a result, Julie will be calling to see us this morning. Does that satisfy your curiosity?" replied Eddie.

"Just asking!" said Maria, with a smirk on her face.

"Ok, let's review the position as of now," said Chief Ned Brennan, as he took his place at the head of the table. "Lennie, what have forensics for us?"

"Well firstly, the toxicology report is in. It shows a high level of alcohol in Newman's blood, plus an unusual cocktail of tablets." replied Lennie. "These included very strong sedatives, sleeping tablets and other tablets of that nature. A deadly cocktail of drugs, according to the report. This would be in keeping with the bottle of mixed tablets we found in his pocket. Strangely, the same mix, although to a much lesser extent, was found in the victim's system."

"Did the report draw any firm conclusions?" asked the Chief.

"Like all such reports, it surmised and postulated with plenty of ifs and buts, but did conclude that the effect on Newman would have been to heighten his senses initially and later on to confuse him and affect his memory somewhat." replied Lennie.

"Great. What exactly, if anything does that tell us?" said the Chief. "And what about the third party that was supposed to have been there? Is there any evidence to substantiate that?"

"We combed the building for prints and the only ones that we found were Gregg Newman's, Tracey's, Angie's and Art Spinks – not another print anywhere." replied Lennie.

"Ok, Eddie, what did you find?" asked the Chief.

"Well, it appears that Newman and Art used the same babysitters and that over the past year at least two of them stopped babysitting for them. That was before Angie started. On each occasion it was Newman who informed Art and in both cases it was Newman who found the replacement."

"Do we know who these sitters are?" asked the Chief.

"Yes, Art has given us the full details and we have plans to interview them after school today. We will advise their parents before we do, as we need them to be present. Also, a friend of Angie's has told us that she knew that Newman gave Angie some substantial presents and that Angie has, or sorry had, kept a diary with specific details of their relationship. We have an appointment with Angie's parents for this morning. Hopefully they will give us the diary, if it exists and if they can locate it." replied Eddie.

"What about the alarm and CCTV?" asked the Chief.

"Well, we were not able to get information from the companies yesterday, it being Sunday, however we have arranged to interview both this morning." said Walt.

"Good," said the Chief, "now all we need to do is to interview Newman. I have spoken to his attorney, Al Mc Nally, and he is agreeable for us to interview him here as long as McNally is present. That is arranged for two thirty this afternoon. So let's get cracking and tidy up the loose ends. We need to nail this quickly."

As they left the incident room Eddie got a call to say that there was a young lady waiting for him at the front desk.

"Hi Julie," said Eddie, as Maria and he approached

the desk. "Thanks for coming in. Now let's see if we can find some privacy."

"I don't think I can give you any more information than I have already given you." began Julie.

"Don't worry about that," said Eddie "I just want to go over what you said so that there can be no confusion later on. So Angie and you were friends, is that so?" said Eddie.

"Yes, on and off, like most school pals. We would confide in each other from time to time." said Julie.

"What kind of things would you confide in for example?" asked Eddie.

"Well when word got out that Gregg Newman was looking for babysitters, I asked Angie what he was like to sit for. She was pretty blunt in what she said, whether it was Tracey I was checking out or Mr Newman. When I quizzed her on what she meant, she inferred that Mr Newman expected certain liberties with his sitters."

"Did she give any explicit information?" asked Eddie.

"Not really, but she did say that on certain nights, she got generous bonuses and that she had it all documented in her diary."

"Did she say where the diary was kept?"

"No, but knowing Angie, she was no fool, she would have it well hidden. All I can say now is how lucky I am not to have been babysitting for him."

As Maria saw Julie to the door, Eddie rang Angie's parents to say that they would be with them in approximately thirty minutes.

"Looks like our Gregg has a problem with young girls," said Eddie, as they drove to Angie's home.

"Yes, it's beginning to look more like a case of accidental homicide or homicide by misadventure than murder one at this stage." replied Maria.

"Well whichever it turns out to be, I think his career is ended," said Eddie.

There were still a number of relatives and neighbors at the house when they called. However, as soon as Eddie and Maria arrived, they made themselves scarce, leaving them with the grieving parents. Having thanked them for agreeing to see them again at short notice and sympathizing with them, Eddie asked them to tell them how Angie ended up babysitting on the Friday evening.

"Well, Angie had been sitting for Mr Newman for almost six months and she would get a text or cell-call. We never knew which. You know what teenagers are like in that regard. So on Friday she just announced that she was going over to Newman's to sit for an hour or two. There was nothing strange about that. It often happened that Mr Newman would be delayed and needed to bridge a short period. He would always pay extra for that. He was a generous man." said Mrs Lummox. Mr Lummox just sat there looking at the floor.

"So we believe," said Maria.

"We hate to impose on you at a time of such grief," said Eddie pressing for information, "but to try and make sense of it all we need to understand everything we can about Mr Newman and to a lesser degree about your daughter. I wonder would it be possible to have a look at her room? It may give us some clue as to why this awful thing has happened to her?"

"I don't know what you would expect to find, but if you think it would help, we have no objections." said Mrs Lummox.

"Sometimes people, especially teenagers leave notes in their schoolbags and some even keep a diary. Did Angie keep a diary?" asked Eddie.

"No, not that I knew of." replied Mrs Lummox.

Angie's room was a typical teenager's room. The walls were adorned with posters of film stars and pop groups in the middle of which was a wall planner with a schedule of her class times clearly marked out.

Also on it was a number of what looked like coded entries. There was a number of 'G' and 'R' and 'S' marked in over the past number of months.

"Have you any idea what these letters refer to?" asked Maria. "Would the 'G' refer to babysitting for Gregg Newman, by any chance?"

"Sorry but I have no idea what any of it could mean," said Mrs Lummox.

While this conversation was going on, Eddie was looking for any obvious, that was, obvious to him, places where Angie would have hidden her diary. Finally, he decided that if it was in the room, the most obvious place would have been on top of her wardrobe. A chair was situated just beside it making it easy to put it there safely and out of reach of Mrs Lummox, who was a small stout woman and who by the look of her, would not be inclined to climb up on chairs.

"Do you mind if I just have a quick look on top of the wardrobe?" asked Eddie.

"Oh my God, it must be full of dust. I'm sure Angie hasn't dusted it since this became her room." replied a flustered Mrs Lummox.

What Eddie found on top of the wardrobe wasn't dust. It was a treasure chest of personal items that Angie kept there. Amongst the items was a very fancy diary, tied with a ribbon.

"This seems to be what we are looking for." said

Eddie as he carefully lifted the diary and placed it in an evidence bag. "Do you mind if we take it with us, I am sure it will help us to find the truth about your daughter?"

"Oh my God, I never knew she kept a diary," said Mrs Lummox. "Of course you can take it. I just couldn't bear to read something like that right now."

When they got back to the station they firstly registered the evidence and then, having donned gloves, carefully opened the diary.

"Wow! Whatever you might say about Angie, she certainly knew how to keep records." said Maria.

"Yep, she sure did." replied Eddie, "Every encounter she had with Gregg Newman, going back since she started babysitting for him, six months ago, is recorded in detail. This is explosive stuff – if we can use it. Here, have a look at the last entry. 'It's over – he is now too important for poor little me'."

Chapter 12

It was a very happy Shirley who headed off to Oldtown on Monday morning. She still hadn't heard from Jeff but had her mind made up to dump him if he did contact her. Her evening with Eddie had been a breath of fresh air.

He was charming and funny and made her feel good, even if he didn't come on heavy with her. She liked that. He said he would call her later on that week and she just knew that he would. They had been completely open with each other, well almost. She told him why she was still single at twenty-eight – a shame according to her mother. Was she ever going to give her grandchildren? Most of her friends were grandparents for years now.

He had told her of his failed marriage, taking responsibility for its failure, putting the job before her needs. Since the divorce eighteen months ago he had stayed away from any kind of serious relationships.

Now she was on her way, with her newfound responsibility, to track down the background on Gregg Newman's wife and family. Once she cleared the city and hit the freeway she headed south along the river bank that separated the city from the rich farmlands and the multi-colored forests that spread to the east. She was like a child in a sweet factory. She was happy.

She eventually found the offices of the Oldtown Chronicle which were situated in a side street off the main street and looked as if they hadn't been painted for at least ten years. The inside looked even more in need of freshening up which could also be said of the elderly lady sitting behind the reception desk.

"Good morning," began Shirley. "I have an appointment to see Mr Harding."

"And who might you be?" replied the receptionist while perusing the diary in front of her. A diary that Shirley could see was empty of appointments, apart from her name.

"My name is Shirley Green. I spoke to Mr Harding on Saturday last." replied Shirley.

"Oh yes, I see it here. Please take a seat and I will advise Mr Harding that you have arrived. He is a very busy man you know." said the receptionist.

Fifteen minutes later, Shirley was lead up two flights of rickety stairs to Mr Harding's office.

Her first impressions were that, like the outside of the building, Mr Harding was much older and decrepit than her boss had led her to believe. He was at least seventy pounds' overweight and had made very little effort to spruce himself up for their meeting. She hoped his memory was better than his appearance.

"Ah, good morning Miss Green," said Mr Harding, "I'm Don – your boss Butch and I go back a long way. We both graduated from the same college and both of us worked here in Oldtown for a year or two before he moved on to the city and bigger things. Now he is in a different league to me. As this town shrunk and all the ambitious ones headed to the city, some of us had to stay and keep the ship afloat, so to speak."

"Thank you very much for seeing me at such short notice, my name is Shirley. I am doing a human interest story on Mr Gregg Newman, whom I hope you will remember from when he lived here in Oldtown."

"Yes, Butch mentioned that you would be asking about one of our more illustrious citizens. Didn't he do well for himself?"

"Well, as you probably heard, he is in a spot of bother at the moment. However, what I am trying to find out is who and what and where is Mrs Newman?" replied Shirley, getting straight to the point.

"Ah yes, Mrs Newman. A very good question. She was a fine looking filly when she came to work here in Oldtown. I think it must have been all of seven or eight years ago. It was a case of bees around the honey pot. All the eligible young ones, and I might add others also wanted her, but she was a sharp country girl who wasn't easily had.

She had ambitions and was very focused on getting what she wanted."

"Can you remember where she came from?"

"No, I'm afraid I never knew exactly where she came from and yet my memory tells me that she was a much grounded country girl. She started work in the local law firm as a secretary and that is where Gregg met her. He was a junior lawyer in the firm."

"Did she have any girlfriends who might know about her family?"

"Again, you are asking my poor memory very hard questions. There was a Mrs Brown who ran a boarding house over on Pine Street at that time and, I could be wrong, but I do believe that Mrs Newman boarded there for a time. However, I can't say for sure if she is still alive or not."

"Can you remember anything about their wedding?"

"Oh yes, catching Gregg Newman was the talk of the town. He thought he was God's answer to every woman's prayer, and acted as if he was. But Alice, yes that was her name, led him a merry dance. If you want me – you marry me. And by God he did."

"From what you say, it must have been a society wedding here in Oldtown. Would you have any reports or photos of the wedding in your archives?"

"We probably have but with the way business has been going and that thing, social media, taking over, we haven't had sufficient business to maintain enough staff to keep things like archival records that up to date. However, since that would have been about ten years ago, we just might have something. I will get Matilda, whom you met in reception, to check."

'With Matilda checking, I won't hold my breath,' thought Shirley. "So what happened to the marriage?" she asked.

"At this stage I think we need to get something to eat," said Dom. "Grab your coat and we will walk around the corner to Teddy's Diner. We can finish our gossip there. I'm hungry."

Teddy's diner consisted of one long room with eight floor to ceiling windows overlooking Main Street. All tables were set in individual booths. Dom led the way to a booth at the furthest end.

When they were seated and had ordered their food, a double cheese burger and fries for Don and a healthy Caesar salad for Shirley, Don said, "You were asking where it all went wrong. Well, I believe it went wrong even before it started."

"How do you mean, even before it started?"

"As I said, Newman was used to getting whatever girl he wanted, on his terms. He wanted Alice as his biggest trophy but he got her on her terms – marriage.

However, it didn't stop his womanizing, once their only child was born. He kept looking at greener pastures. At that stage the state Democratic Party machine had their eyes on him and was grooming him, as a very creditable future elections candidate, and more. The committee comprised the likes of ex-judge Leo Forrest, local attorney Al McNally, and Teddy Moran, chairman of the Local Farmers Bank. They were serious about the image they wanted Newman to adopt."

"So Newman's wandering eyes didn't fit in too well with their plan."

"Definitely not. Rumours of shouting matches in the Newman house became commonplace, as Alice confronted Gregg on his infidelities. On a few occasions the police were called by concerned neighbors but on each occasion no charges were made by Alice."

"So what happened to her?"

"Well, the facts as I knew the and now remember them, was that it all came to a head one evening up at the Country Club. Gregg was attending a Democratic Party fundraiser when Alice stormed in, apparently intoxicated, shouting at Gregg that he had stooped to a new low by having sex with their fifteen-year-old babysitter."

"Wow, that put the cat amongst the pigeons, I would think."

"It certainly did. Security was called and she was quickly removed. No one seemed to know for sure what exactly happened after that. Word had it that she had a nervous breakdown and was hospitalized upstate. She then seemed to have faded out of the picture until a year or so later when I remember hearing that Newman had divorced her, getting custody of the daughter."

"But somebody must know what happened. Surely she must have had family or close friends who would know?"

"As I said, the circle she and Newman moved in was much politicized and she didn't make real friends, if you know what I mean. As regards family, I got the impression that she was very much on her own."

"Do you think the local hospital would talk to me? There must be some record of her whereabouts."

"Listen Shirley, if the people involved in her hospitalization didn't want people to know where she was, they knew how to ensure that Alice didn't embarrass Newman or the Party ever again. You can bet your bottom dollar on that. In the meantime, you might call to the town hall. They should have records of the wedding and divorce, I presume."

"Thanks Don for seeing me and giving me so much of your time. Here let me get the check," said Shirley, fumbling with her purse.

"Not at all, you don't realize how much it means to an old guy like me to be of interest to someone as young as you. And as for time, I have plenty of that at the moment. It has been a pleasure. You can tell Butch that if he ever has no work for you, we would love to have you here in Oldtown. In the meantime, I will get Matilda to check the archival system and send you on whatever she finds. Drive safely."

Chapter 13

Tension was high in the incident room as the Chief, Ned Brennan and the DA, Mary Donnelly, prepared for the arrival of Gregg Newman and his attorney, Al McNally.

Gregg Newman had been discharged from hospital that morning and rather than have the police bring him to the station for questioning, his attorney immediately advised the Chief that Newman would voluntarily be presenting himself at the station for questioning. Both the Chief and the DA were acutely aware of the sensitivity of the situation, one false move and it could jeopardize the case, a case that appeared to be 'open and shut'. The only question was what to charge him with – accidental homicide, first degree murder, or involuntary homicide. The evidence they had to date would seem to indicate a sex game that had gone wrong and therefore the charge should be accidental homicide. There was no evidence of premeditated killing and so that ruled murder out. The only other question was the possibility of involuntary homicide, if what they were doing was deemed to be illegal. Both were happy that Detective Eddie McGrane and Detective Maria Diego would be doing the interview. Both were experienced officers.

As promised, at precisely two thirty p.m. Al McNally and a very disheveled looking Gregg Newman walked into the station and were immediately shown in to the interview room. Gone were the well combed black curly hair and the immaculate dress of Mr Newman. His appearance was that of a person who was deflated. The arrogant strut was no longer in evidence.

"Good afternoon Mr Newman and Mr McNally," said Eddie, shaking hands with both men as he showed them to their seats. "This is my partner, Maria Diego. Can I get you some coffee?"

"Thank you," said Al, speaking for both of them, "we would appreciate that."

Once the coffee had been served and the interview got under way, Al McNally said that he wanted it to go on record that Gregg Newman had voluntarily presented himself at the police station in order to help with the investigation.

"Thank you Mr McNally, that is duly recorded," said Eddie, who then proceeded to read Gregg Newman his rights. Having done that, Eddie began.

"Mr Newman, the purpose of this interview is to establish what exactly led to the death of Miss Angie Lummox on Friday the 10th of October last, at your home, 45 Elm Grove. Perhaps you would begin by telling us of the events of that evening, prior to you arriving at your home and why you asked Miss Lummox to call to your home."

"Well, if I can start by categorically denying that I asked Miss Lummox to call to my house, and then we can get that lie out of the way." replied Gregg.

"Mr Newman, the record of Miss Lummox's cell phone shows a text message from you asking her to be at your home six thirty, as usual. That the alarm would be off and the key would be in the usual place. These records are fact, Mr Newman." countered Eddie.

"They may be facts on Miss Lummox's phone but they are not on my cell phone." Gregg barked, as he pulled his expensive iPhone out of his pocket.

"Sorry, Mr Newman but we are not referring to that phone. We are talking about the other phone that you have," said Eddie taking a simple pay-as-you-go cell phone out of his file. "This phone is registered in your name, or do you deny this also?"

"But I lost that phone some months ago," exclaimed Gregg.

"Oh you lost it, did you? And I suppose you reported that to your phone company, did you? Did you even think to look in your bedside locker drawer? Where we found it?"

"No, I didn't. I didn't think it was completely lost. I assumed that I had mislaid it somewhere in the house. You see, I didn't use it very often." Gregg replied.

"Maybe you just used it to arrange your babysitters."

"That is ridiculous. Why would I keep a separate phone for that? Even if I did use another phone to arrange a babysitter, which I didn't. Is that some kind of crime now?"

"Ok, when our officer spoke to you on Friday evening, you talked about being stung by something like a Taser gun and muttered that you had one yourself. However, we can find no trace of it anywhere and there isn't any evidence of it anywhere in the house. Where exactly did you store this 'Taser gun' you talk about and if you did possess one, why did you?"

"I bought it years ago for my own protection when I lived in Oldtown. Security wasn't as good there as it is here. I always kept it in a floor safe under my desk. Check that and you will see."

"That's very interesting, Mr Newman. When we asked your attorney to see the contents of your safe, he never mentioned the existence of a second 'secret' safe. What else is in it?" asked Eddie.

"Just some private papers and my 'lawfully' held gun."

"Ok, let's leave that for the present. We will need

the code in order to verify that. In the meantime, bring us through what you did between five thirty p.m. and six thirty p.m. on Friday last."

"At approximately four p.m. I was in the Jazz bar on Townsend Street, having a few celebratory drinks with a number of my colleagues. Here is a list of their names, they will corroborate that. I then headed home to collect my daughter from my neighbor Mr Spinks and his wife Lucy, who had collected her from school along with their own daughter Jenny. I was due to collect her between seven p.m. and seven thirty p.m. I arrived home at approximately five forty-five p.m."

"Did you notice anything strange or different when you arrived at the house or anybody in the vicinity?"

"I have been thinking about that and the only thing I was aware of was that the security light didn't come on – again. This had happened a few times in the past month and I had reported it. Other than that, everything seemed normal to me."

"Ok, so having parked your car, what happened next?"

"I opened the door and stepped into the hall and just sensed someone coming up behind me and pushing something against my shoulder before I could turn. I then apparently blacked out and when I came to I was aware of somebody giving me something to drink and then the pain in my shoulder again."

"When you entered your house, Mr Newman, do you remember turning off the alarm?" asked Eddie.

"Now that you mention it, no I don't. In fact, I couldn't have had time to do anything. I don't even recall turning on the light."

"So you are telling us that, firstly, you didn't turn off the alarm? A sophisticated alarm that, according to the alarm company had been properly deactivated at one thirty p.m. Something that their records show happen on a regular Friday afternoon. And secondly, that you didn't turn on any light and yet you claim to have sensed a person come up behind you. Is that your story?"

"Yes, as far as I can recall. I am still suffering from the effects of what has happened, as I am sure you will appreciate."

"Well, let me help you recall what happened. We have traced the text that the deceased young girl got that afternoon at one thirty-five p.m. and it came from your phone which we found in your bedside drawer, with your, and only your, fingerprints on it."

"But that can't be," exclaimed Gregg. "I was working on Friday last. My colleagues can vouch for that."

"That's funny. None of them can vouch for your

whereabouts for the lunchtime period of approximately one p.m. to two p.m."

"But of course they can't! I went for my usual lunchtime jog."

"Do you not find it a bit of a coincidence that your house alarm was deactivated at one thirty p.m., a message to the deceased was sent from your second phone at one thirty-five p.m. A phone that has only your fingerprints on it? Incidentally we will have the full content of all your calls, shortly. Do you really expect anyone to believe that? Listen Gregg, let's not waste any more time. Do you want to tell us exactly what happened? And, let me add, we know that this particular liaison has been going on for quite some time."

At that time Al McNally intervened to request a recess so that he could confer with his client.

"Before we do that," said Eddie, "can you tell us where Mrs Newman is?"

"As you must know, Mrs Newman and I were divorced some years ago in an uncontested action. The judge found in my favor giving me sole custody of my daughter. Since then I have had no contact with her and have absolutely no idea where she went or for that matter, where she is now," replied Gregg.

Chapter 14

"Gregg, I can't defend you if you don't level with me!" pleaded Al as soon as Gregg and he had privacy. "I need the truth, Gregg. And I mean the whole truth. Let's start with your babysitter. Were you having some kind of sexual relationship with her? Did you have an arrangement to meet her in your house last Friday?"

"Look Al, my relationships with women are my business. I am single and Angie was of age, so I am entitled to my privacy. So yes, I did arrange to meet her on Friday. It was a regular meeting. But that is where it ends. I did not tie her up and kill her. You better believe me Al!"

"Shit, Gregg!" said Al. "What were you thinking of? This is going from bad to worse. I believe that unless you can come up with a reasonable explanation, they are going to charge you today with either murder or accidental homicide. If they do that and even if later on, we win the case, one way or another you are finished. I need to know all of the facts."

"But Al, I didn't do it. There must be some proof that there was a third party in my house. I'm not just dreaming this up."

"OK, go back and tell me again. How you would

arrange to meet Miss Lummox." said Al.

"Usually, I would take a jog on Fridays and come in the back entrance to my house. I would then deactivate the alarm and call Angie to tell her what time to be at the house later that evening. She knew where the key would be hidden and the alarm would be off. When we were finished, she would leave by the back way. No one would ever see us together."

"So while all of that gives you cover for entering and exiting your house, without being observed, it also would give a third party complete cover. If what you are telling me is true, then your attention to detail would also have covered any intruder. We will have to work on that issue."

"There must be something we can do. We have to. The election is less than three weeks away."

"I am only too well aware of that. The committee had a meeting to plan their strategy. I can tell you they are not a happy lot right now. You have really left them in the shit."

"Surely, with your influence with the DA you can get her to defer charges until after the elections, pending your investigations."

"Ok, let's get back in and I will see how confident they are in their case."

While the interview was taking place, the Chief Ned

and Mary the DA were carefully observing the proceedings. During the recess, the Chief said "It looks to me that we have a clear cut case of accidental homicide. What do you think, Mary?"

"Well Chief, it is not always that easy to decide in a case like this. Yes, we apparently have an open and shut case. But what the charge is to be is very important. I would like to get more advice before deciding on it." replied Mary.

"So what is the specific difference?" asked Ned.

"The law states that, and I quote:

Accidental killing means a death caused by an act which is lawful and lawfully done under a reasonable belief that no harm is possible. Accidental killing is different from involuntary manslaughter, which is the result of an unlawful act or of a lawful act done in an unlawful way. However, an accidental killing committed in the course of an unlawful, or felonious act, constitutes involuntary manslaughter.

The Common Law of Crimes distinguishes two types of accidental killings. They are accidental killings resulting from unlawful acts of violence not directed at the victim, and accidental killings resulting from lawful acts of violence. The first type was punishable as manslaughter and the second type were excusable as homicide by misadventure.

It could be argued that what Newman and Angie were up to was consensual sex play and that her death was an accident that arose from that. Therefore, the charge should be accidental death. However, it could just as easily be argued that the placing of his belt around Angie's throat was outside the bounds of sex play and therefore the charge would be of manslaughter."

"Ok, in that case we had better not press charges until we are absolutely sure. That means that we will see Al McNally pull his client out now." said the Chief.

Sure enough, on returning to the interview room, Al declared. "It is obvious that someone is setting my client up. He is totally innocent of any charge you might think up. We absolutely refute your insinuations, for that is all they are. I am instructing my client to adopt the Fifth Amendment and refuse to answer any further questions on the grounds that he may incriminate himself. So unless you intend to charge him, good day to you."

With that they both got up and left the room.

Chapter 15

"Are these the only records you have?" Shirley enquired of the clerk in the town hall, who was busy shuffling papers.

"Sorry ma'am, but I can't manufacture records that don't exist, even for a pretty face like yours," replied the clerk.

"So, a marriage certificate dated eight years ago for the marriage of Mr Gregg Newman and Miss Alice Mason, both with Oldtown addresses, and a similar record dated five years later in relation to an uncontested divorce, with sole custody of their daughter being given to Mr Gregg Newman. That's it?" said Shirley.

"As I said ma'am, I just work here. I don't make up the information."

'So much for the mysterious Alice Newman,' thought Shirley as she headed for Pine Street to see if she could track down a boarding house run by a Mrs Brown. Parking the car at the southern end of the street she began to check all the houses on the right-hand side of the street, with no luck. It was halfway down the left-hand side that she noticed an old lady weeding her garden.

"Excuse me ma'am," said Shirley "I am looking for a Mrs Brown who used to run a boarding house in this street about ten years ago. Would you possibly know which house was hers?"

"And who might you be?" asked the old lady. Suspicion in her face.

"Well, my name is Shirley Green and I work for a TV station up in the city and I am doing a human interest story on a Mr Gregg Newman and in particular, on his wife Alice. Apparently Alice boarded with this Mrs Brown, before she married Mr Newman." replied Shirley.

"Well, well, poor Alice," said the old lady "She was a lovely girl and a perfect lodger. She stayed with me for about two years and then she went off and married that good for nothing lawyer fellow, Gregg Newman. Oh by the way, I am that Mrs Brown you are looking for. Please call me Kaley. Do come in and we can chat over a cup of coffee."

"Oh thank you, I would love to," said Shirley.

"Just you sit there, young lady and I will put the kettle on." said Kaley as she busied herself in the kitchen. While she was doing that, Shirley decided to text Eddie. She had been itching to do it all day but didn't want to seem too interested. After all they had had only one evening out and that didn't end with anything more than an airbrush cheek to cheek. But she felt there was more to come and really enjoyed his humour and his normality. He wasn't out for a quick rumble in the bed, otherwise he would have made a move on Saturday night last. No, he was definitely different from the usual bunch of halfwits that were to be found in every bar and disco in the city.

'Hi Eddie, hope you are having a good day!' she texted 'Trying to trace Gregg Newman's wife here in Oldtown is like trying to unravel a ball of wool that the cat had been playing with. I think I am going to have to ask you for help. Call me when you get a chance.' Before she had time to reflect and change the text, she pressed, send.

'Oh God, I hope I haven't put my foot in it. I shouldn't have asked him to ring me. What will he think?' thought Shirley. However, before she could further analyses what she had done, Kaley arrived in with a pot of coffee and some cookies.

"Now," said Kaley when she had poured the coffee. "Let's talk about Alice."

"Well perhaps you know something about her background, where she came from, what her parents were like, how many sisters and brothers she had. Anything like that. I am trying to get to understand her as a person. Unfortunately, very few here in Oldtown know much about her or just won't talk. She appears to have no past, and now, no future. She seems to have just disappeared into thin air."

Shirley had hit the jackpot. Mrs Brown knew everyone in Oldtown, and more importantly, she wanted to talk about them – all of them. That was the problem, trying to keep her focus on Alice Newman.

It appeared that Mrs Brown, 'call me Kaley', and Alice had become very good friends during the period she was lodging there. However, once they got married Newman kept a tight rein on her social life. She was now an appendage to the up and coming Mr Gregg Newman, a man who intended going places.

"I suppose I would really call Alice a straight talking, fun loving, but very ambitious dear girl. It took me a long time to gain her confidence when she came to live with me. At first she would spend most of her time in her room. She later told me she was planning her future in detail. It was the one thing that upset me. She was so mercenary in that regard. Then she became obsessed with fitness and even used to give yoga lessons to some of her work colleagues."

"Did she talk much about her parents?"

"Eventually, between what she would say and what I surmised, I understand that she was an only child. I remember her telling me that while she was away at college, her parents split up, very acrimoniously, and as soon as Alice graduated she moved to Oldtown and never went back to either parent."

"Wow. That was some statement. She must have been a very strong and independent young girl."

"She was an enigma. Outwardly she was the stunningly beautiful girl without an apparent care in the world. Inside she was the ultimate schemer. But I loved her dearly. When she got married I was heartbroken. I had lost a confidante and only once did she come back to visit me. That was before she got sick."

"You're the second person to mention her sickness. What exactly happened?"

"As I mentioned, Alice moved up in society once she married Gregg. As a result, I heard very little about her other than newspaper reports of social events at which she and Gregg would feature prominently. You can imagine then how I felt when one of the caterers up at the Country Club told me, one morning, that Alice was in hospital."

"Did she say why she was there?"

"There were many rumours. Some said she had a drink problem, others said she had some kind of breakdown, due to over work. My view was that it was the stress of living with that no good Gregg. Apparently Alice had confronted Gregg in the Country Club about sleeping with their babysitter."

"Wow! So what happened then?"

"As soon as I heard that, I headed straight up to the

hospital only to be told that she was no longer there. The story was that she had been moved for specialist treatment to a clinic upstate and they were not at liberty to comment further."

"But surely someone must have talked about her whereabouts?"

"Of course they did, but they weren't saying what exactly the full story was. I pestered Gregg, calling his phone and even calling to his office. Not once had he the decency to meet me or answer my phone calls. On the contrary, I got a letter from his law firm accusing me of harassing Mr Newman and advising me of the consequence if I didn't stop calling."

"They actually threatened you?"

"You better believe it! When it comes to politics, these people are ruthless."

"So what happened then?"

"She just disappeared. Some months later I saw a two-inch snippet in the local newspaper to the effect that Mr Gregg Newman and Mrs Alice Newman had divorced, that was all. I have never heard of her since."

"Kaley, would you be prepared to do a short interview on NTTV? Just outlining what you have just told me. We can coach you if you feel nervous and there would be a small fee." Shirley asked, trying to remain calm.

"Well, I suppose I could but I would need to have something done with my hair and of course what would I wear?"

"Don't you worry a bit about that? I will arrange for the cameraman to be here at 3.00p.m. I will do the interview myself. You will look smashing. Let me make a quick phone call back to the station."

Having persuaded Butch to send down a cameraman with the promise of a breakthrough in the search for Mrs Newman, she set about scripting the interview. The main focus was to be on the reason for the breakup of the marriage, the accusation that Newman had been sleeping with their babysitter. This tied in nicely with the current case against him and it was Shirley's exclusive. Things were looking good.

"'I need to talk to Eddie McGrane soon. To share the good news.' Shirley mused. She had at last put some flesh on Alice Newman, the woman.

The interview took all of fifteen minutes and by the time it was edited it was just five minutes long. Kaley did brilliantly recounting her early days with the beautiful Alice who came to lodge with her and then on to her social climb with her new husband Gregg Newman. She covered the rumours that she had heard of the incident in the Country Club without mentioning specific people. Yet the message was perfectly clear. She had dared to publicly confront Newman in relation to his relationship with a young babysitter and that ended her marriage.

Butch was ecstatic. Once again he praised Shirley for her initiative and her growing ability to handle a very tricky interview situation. The interview would be shown on the nine o'clock news under the heading 'developments in the ongoing investigation of the tragic death of Miss Angie Lummox at the home of Mr Gregg Newman.'

Chapter 16

The Chief had just had another call from City Hall. If you are going to charge him, do it now. We need to be seen to be on top of this case. Remember Gregg Newman is a candidate for the mayoral elections in two weeks' time. We need action, was the clear message.

"Can we use the diary as evidence?" asked the Chief.

"Again, in so far as it was voluntarily given to us by the victim's parents I believe we can. But, if it is contested, and it may be, I couldn't guarantee that it would be upheld in court." replied Mary Donnelly.

"On what grounds could it be contested?"

"Well, we would have to prove that it was her diary and that all the contents were in her writing. It could get tricky."

"But we do have someone who will state that Angie told her about her diary. If she were to confirm that, would that not do?"

"Yes and no. These things are never straight forward and in most cases it comes down to the presiding judge and how he or she sees it." Mary frowned as she considered the risks.

"One other thing that we discovered when we opened

Newman's floor safe, he was obviously a very detailed man and insisted on all of his babysitters completing a job application form. One of the questions on it was date of birth. He knew exactly what their ages were."

The Chief paused, "So, the question is, can we arrest him and charge him in connection with the unlawful killing of Miss Angie Lummox. If so, then we need to have him arraigned before a judge on that basic count. Is that right? We can then add charges in connection with having sex with a minor. Do we all agree with that?" asked the Chief.

"I never can understand why some states have fifteen years of age consent and here we have an eighteen-year age limit." sighed Mary. "I know we tried to have it repealed two years ago, but we were defeated. In my view, that was a purely political decision. But yes, that is a fair summary, I say we go with it. I will ring Judge Quiril and see when he is free to sit."

"Good, and when you arrange the time it might be prudent to advise Mr McNally of what is happening before we arrest Newman."

While they were waiting for the time to go and arrest Newman, Eddie was busy checking his cell phone and spotted the text from Shirley. Funnily, he had just been thinking of her.

"Hi there, and what can I do for you?" began Eddie when Shirley answered his call. "Don't tell me you are lost in that hick town of Oldtown!"

"Well, for your information, I have had a very productive day chasing the elusive Mrs Newman. Furthermore, Mister Detective, what I found out might be of interest to you!" Shirley teased. "Watch the nine o'clock news tonight. I have just interviewed a lady who knew Alice Newman and who will state that the breakup of the marriage was due to Mrs Newman confronting Newman in public about sleeping with their babysitter. Does that ring a bell?"

"Now that sounds intriguing," said Eddie, "For your information, and yours only, that person will be brought to the courthouse later this evening, to be charged with the death of Angie Lummox. That should be no later than seven p.m. After that I would be free for some badly needed food. Care to join me?"

"When you beg like that? How could I refuse?" laughed Shirley.

As soon as she got off of the phone, she immediately called Butch.

"Well, well, well. If it isn't our intrepid investigator!" began Butch, "And what more great news have you unearthed now, might I ask?"

"Apart from having substantial success in uncovering the real Mrs Newman, of which I have just enlightened you, I am sure you would like to get a camera crew over to meet me at the courthouse. Mr Gregg Newman will be arrested and brought there to be arraigned sometime around seven p.m. Before you ask, I can't divulge my source, as well you know." replied Shirley.

"Are you sure?" asked Butch.

"Only one way to find out! Make sure we have a camera there. I will head straight there." replied Shirley. She wasn't about to let anyone else steal her show! Immediately she headed for home to shower and make herself presentable for her next TV appearance.

Meanwhile, back in the station, Mary Donnelly had managed to contact Judge Quiril just as he was about to head out to the theatre. He immediately agreed to sit at six thirty p.m. The fact that he was a Republican appointee just may have swayed his decision.

"Ok Eddie," said the Chief, "make sure all the paperwork is in order and that he is properly advised of his rights. Then bring him in. Just keep it low-key. No blaring sirens or flashing lights."

"Hi Mr McNally," said Mary. "Just giving you a heads up. We are going to charge Mr Newman in connection with the death of Angie Lummox and be aware we may have some additional charges to add later. We won't oppose bail but between you and me, it does not look good for Newman. We also understand that NTTV have uncovered some details of Newman's past and they will be aired on tonight's nine o'clock news. Before you ask, we have no details of the content of the piece. You do know however that since the incident, they have been keeping the issue alive with historical snippets every evening. They must have an issue with the Democratic Party!"

Al McNally immediately rang Leo Forrest, chairman of the Party Election Committee. "Time to pull the plug. I haven't advised him yet, but he will be arraigned before Judge Quiril at around about six thirty p.m." he said. "I will get to the meeting as soon as the hearing is over."

By the time Eddie and Maria arrived at Newman's house he was waiting for them. Al, having advised him of what was coming down for him. As advised by Al, he made no comment when Eddie formally arrested him and charged him in connection with the death of Miss Angie Lummox. When they got to the courthouse they were surprised to find the NTTV van parked strategically outside.

"Damn it, how did they find out?" exclaimed Eddie, reddening. "I think there is a back entrance. Hopefully it is open."

However, they were out of luck. It was closed so they had to return to the front entrance. Then in the full glare of the cameras they quickly ushered Newman inside.

The court hearing took precisely ten minutes. Having heard Eddie giving details of the charge and arrest on behalf of the state, Judge Quiril asked if the state had any objection to bail being granted. Mary Donnelly replied that they had no objection. Bail was set at $10,000 and it was hoped that the case would be heard early in the New Year.

While Al McNally was Gregg Newman's attorney, he was no criminal defense lawyer, never having defended a client in a criminal case, let alone a possible murder case. In addition, as part of the group who had Alice committed, he had a personal conflict of interest. Newman had instructed him to employ the best defense lawyer available while agreeing, under any circumstances, not to bring up his suspicions that his wife was involved in the incident. A difficult task, but not an impossible one for Al. He knew the man he wanted, Joe Breslin. A man with a reputation for getting witnesses to begin to doubt their own names.

He also owed Al a favor. Time to collect.

The following day, having introduced Joe to Gregg, Al left the room and washed his hands of the case.

"Ok, start at the beginning and tell me your story." said Joe.

An hour later, Gregg said, "That's it in a nutshell, I didn't do it. Full stop. Someone set me up."

"Any idea who that might be?"

"Not really, but I assume it was someone who didn't want me to win the election. Who knows?"

"Let's leave the issue of the charges out for the moment. If what you say is true, then someone who knows you very intimately had to have access to your home and to your safes. Do you have any family that would have that kind of access?" asked Joe.

"No, I live with my eight-year-old daughter and she would not have any knowledge of, for example, my floor safe."

"Would any of your babysitters have that kind of knowledge?"

"Absolutely no way."

"So that leaves the possibility of an outside source being involved and if that is the case, they must have had you under surveillance for some time and to do that someone must have seen something, everyone leaves a trail. We will concentrate on that immediately. Because the police are so sure of their case they may have only questioned the neighbors on what they may have seen on the Friday at issue."

"But how could someone be in my house and not leave some evidence of having been there?"

"That is exactly what the prosecution will be hammering home to the jury and we must be able to rebut it, or at the very least, cast doubts on the validity of that evidence."

"What about the charges?"

"Well, we will have to challenge both charges on the basis of consensual sex between adults resulting in accidental death. But that's down the road. Let me get to work and I will be checking in with you every other day."

Chapter 17

Leo Forrest puffed angrily on a fat Cuban cigar, his favorite, but he was getting very little satisfaction from it this evening.

"What in the name of God was he doing?" he said to the four other members of the committee, as they sat in his office on the Monday evening.

"He was doing what he always did," said Teddy Moran, who always held that they had picked the wrong man to contest the election. "A leopard never changes his spots as my mother always said. We should have dumped him four years ago. Now what do we do?"

"We do what we always do. We stand fast." retorted Mark Reilly. "He is not guilty until proven guilty."

"What do you think Al?" asked Leo.

"In my view, we have a very serious situation here. The evidence against Gregg looks conclusive. He will be found guilty of at least accidental homicide and I believe they have further evidence of his lifestyle that will be damning. I really think that we don't have a choice. We must get him to withdraw his candidacy on the basis of ill-health. The case won't be heard for at least two months so it won't be an issue for the election if we dump him now.

In the meantime, we use our usual influence with the press to keep the coverage minimal." Al advised.

"So who do we nominate in his place?" asked Teddy Moran, "Do we have a creditable replacement?"

"Well, if you remember, when we selected Gregg, it was a close call between him and Erin Sullivan." Leo suggested. "I believe she would be the perfect replacement. She is talented, personable, and the fact that we have chosen a female is going to give the press a new angle to get hot over."

"Let me talk to Gregg before we do anything rash." said Al. "He is not going to take this lightly."

"I think we are beyond worrying if Gregg is upset or not. This is his bucket of shit that we are trying to sort out." snapped Leo. "I say we have run out of time. We act now and try and salvage some of the ground we are losing. All in favor raise your hand."

All except Al raised their hand. "I agree that we have to act urgently, but I do think we owe it to Gregg to talk to him first. However, I accept the majority decision," said Al.

"Ok, Al, you advise Gregg." urged Leo. "I will contact Erin. Mark you make out the statement for the press and arrange a press conference for first thing tomorrow morning. Teddy, you get the posters printed and the volunteers ready to be mobilized to remove Gregg's and replace them with Erin's. Let's go. We have a mammoth task ahead of us."

Next morning Al called to see Gregg and check on how he was progressing with Joe Breslin.

"Look, Gregg, you have left the committee with no alternative. For the Party's sake and for your own sake, it is best if you withdraw your name. That way you will get another chance." Al pleaded, as he tried to convince Gregg to withdraw before being forcibly removed by the Party.

"Do you think I am guilty, Al?" said Gregg. "Because if you do, then you are wasting my time. However, if you think I am not, which I am not, then how could you even suggest that I withdraw? The case won't be heard until well after the election by which time the incident will be old hat."

"This isn't just about you and me, Gregg. The Party have put everything into this election. They don't intend to lose again this time. Even if the trial hasn't taken place the public will see it one way – you are guilty in the eyes of the electorate! Did you see this morning's newspapers? 'Sex Orgy at Elm Grove' being one of the less offensive headlines. The press is just getting a smell of scandal. God alone knows what NTTV will have on their news bulletin tonight."

"Let them say what they want. I know the truth. I have never tied up a girl in my life, so why would I do it now?" said Gregg.

"Listen Gregg, the Party thinks the world of you, but they call the final shots and I am afraid that today they have called you out. Erin Sullivan will be your replacement. We need you to make a statement to the press to the effect that, as a result of the tragic event that took place in your home, you are withdrawing your name from the election. You will also endorse Erin Sullivan."

"All neatly wrapped up. And when am I to make this announcement?"

"There will be a press conference tomorrow morning at ten a.m. in Leo's office. We need you there looking good and we will have the announcement ready for you," replied Al.

Chapter 18

"So how was your trip to Oldtown?" Eddie asked, as he picked Shirley up at her apartment.

"Do you really want to know or is this your latest pickup line?" Shirley replied.

"You really are sharp. I have been working for hours on that pickup line and you saw straight through it. Ok, first things first. How hungry are you and have you any preference as to where we dine?"

"Well, I haven't had a proper meal all day, and so I could murder a medium steak and fries. I am abstaining from vegetarianism for the moment, if that is alright with you?"

"Perfect, just what I was thinking also. Nemo's is the place to be. While it specializes in fish food, I don't know any other restaurant that can produce such a perfect steak – every time."

As he negotiated the evening traffic, he was aware of how he had been looking forward, all day, to meeting her again. There was something very natural about her that attracted him to her. She was the complete opposite to Olive, his ex-wife. Now she was something else. Full of complexities and uncertainties like a rose, he often thought, beautiful, but full of thorns. Shirley, on the other hand, was no film star but had a beautiful smile which she used unsparingly. He got the impression that she was not out to impress in any way, and had a mind of her own but not an arrogant one.

Even though it was a Monday evening, Nemo's looked exceptionally busy. Eddie was pleased that he had booked a table. He knew that no matter what Shirley's choice of food was; Nemo's would be able to cater for it.

The minute they entered, Eddie was welcomed with a warm hug from a very Italian looking head waiter. "Hi Eddie, where you been? We missed you at the Poker game last night. Tommy took us all to the cleaners."

"Sorry I couldn't be there Pete, but all leave is suspended until we get a handle on this incident over in Elm Grove."

"Yes I heard that. So who is this beautiful lady?"

"Pete. be very nice to this lady and keep your hands and eyes off of her. She works for NTTV and just might give your restaurant a good report if you behave," Eddie said with a laugh.

"Of course, Eddie, I make a joke. As always," he said as he led them to a secluded table by the window looking out on the lake.

"Well detective Eddie, firstly, thanks for the tip off. My

boss seems to think I have a brilliant future with the station. That's today's bulletin. On Friday he was suggesting I find another home for my lack of talents. Oh how fickle are the minds of men, especially TV bosses." Shirley sighed.

"And talking of men. What's the latest position on that boyfriend of yours? You know the one who likes fishing." Eddie probed, as they perused the menu.

"Oh, the bold Jeff is no more. He has bitten the dust. Would you believe, he never once contacted me over the weekend and he had the cheek to text me, not call me, to say that he would be over tonight for 'coffee and a cuddle' no less."

"So does that mean that you are free?"

"No, I am never free. Reasonable yes, free no."

"I was only asking, just in case I heard of someone who might be interested in dating a TV Star." Eddie replied. "And speaking of TV stars, tell me all about your trip to Oldtown, a place I have been to only once, many years ago when it was a thriving town."

"Well, as I mentioned to you on Sunday, I have been given the task of putting flesh on Newman's family. Most people just know the politicians profile. That carefully manicured image that has been looking down on us from the election posters. So, who is Tracey's mother? Who was Gregg Newman's wife, and where can she be now? That's my brief and so far it is very interesting." Shirley replied.

"Wherever she is, I think she is lucky to be away from the mess he is in now. Do you think it wise to point the spotlight on her now? Who knows, she is probably remarried with a clutch of kids, none of whom will thank NTTV for revealing what Newman has done," suggested Eddie.

"I didn't know that police men had consciences, you just put the baddies away. Now I have a moral dilemma." Shirley mused.

"Only if you have found out that what Newman has done would actually impact on her life. Until you find her and I assume that so far you haven't, you are only accumulating information. It is what you do with that information that will count from a moral point of view."

"Let me quickly fill you in on what I have discovered, so far. Then we will talk about you. Ok?"

"Shirley, I hate to bring business into our night out but, do you have all of that on tape by any chance?"

"Of course I do. I'm a professional, you know."

"I never doubted you for a minute. So what happened next?"

"Well, this is where I need your help. It appears that she was hospitalized in the local hospital. The record is there, but that is where it ends. I have been told that she was sent to a psychiatric facility but no one knows, or won't say, where. Then a short time later there is an entry in the local newspaper saying that Newman had divorced with sole custody of the child. I have checked the records in the town hall and they confirm it. Unfortunately, the only address given on the record is the address of where they both lived. According to my sources, big people were involved in all of this. Newman was the Party's golden boy and they didn't want him tarnished."

"Ok, leave it with me and I will follow it up in the morning. Now, red or white wine for the lady?"

By the end of the evening, having had a superb meal, she could not recall exactly what she had eaten. She had found Eddie oh-so-easy to get along with that she felt that she had known him all her life and not someone she had only met once before. She also knew that Eddie had more than a business interest in her, call it woman's intuition.

As he helped her on with her coat as they were leaving the restaurant, he whispered in her ear. "Don't get used to this treatment, Shirley. I'm only trying to make a good impression for the other customers."

"Don't worry, I think you could be easily house trained. If you had the right woman to train you!"

"I suppose this means that I will have to see you again, does it?"

"Oh Eddie, you are so romantic. Did anyone ever tell you that?" Shirley jibed as she linked him back to his car, where, with a flourish, he opened the door for her to get in.

"What a gentleman." Shirley teased.

"Don't push your luck, Miss." Eddie warned her.

When they got to Shirley's apartment, she enquired, as Eddie walked her to her door, "Would you like to come in for a nightcap?"

"I would love to, but I have an early morning briefing session with the Chief and I'd be afraid that if I come in you might have a difficulty in getting me to go home. I had a lovely evening Shirley. Thank you for being the right person at the right time for me."

With that he kissed her gently and almost ran back to his car. "I'll call you tomorrow," he shouted back.

Shirley almost glided into her apartment. She was in love and no doubt about it. Even the phone message from Butch asking her why she did not show up at the courthouse and instructing her to be in his office at nine a.m., the following morning, couldn't bring her back to earth. Life was good once again. This warranted a call to her mother. To tell her that she had met Mr Right. She knew that this would cheer her up.

Chapter 19

"Good work on the Newman case," said the Chief to Eddie and Maria as they sat in his office on the Tuesday morning. "We'll need to copper-fasten all of our interviews and make sure that there are no sudden monkeys jumping out of the bag. But first I want you to liaise with Traffic in relation to that awful accident last Friday evening on the freeway. They seem a little unclear as to how it happened. Just have a look."

"If I didn't know better, I would think that we are being put on Traffic." said Maria, as they headed for the Traffic section.

"Don't even joke about it." Eddie said. "The guy we are going to meet is an old colleague of mine, Bill Jonson. When I joined the force he was my lieutenant and a nicer and more professional boss you will not meet.

Unfortunately, the car he was driving was rammed by a gang as they were trying to escape from a botched bank raid and he lost a leg. When he returned to duty he was assigned to Traffic and has been there for the past three years."

While the Traffic section was located in the same

building, to get to it they had to leave the main block and enter a separate entrance one hundred yards up the street. Such was the shambolic layout of the station. In the Chief's view, the entire block needed to be knocked and rebuilt. He didn't hold out much hope for that.

"Hi Bill, this is my partner, Maria Diego." said Eddie, as they entered Bill Jonson's office.

"Now, tell us about the accident up at the clinic. The Chief tells me you have doubts and if you have doubts I know you long enough to believe that you have good reason. Tell us what's going on in your mind, Bill."

"First things first, let's get us a pot of coffee. I hate that dishwater that they call coffee that the dispenser in the lobby produces."

When they were settled around the table, Bill said, "I'm sure you heard all about the accident. Three people killed and twelve injured and ten vehicles written off. It was carnage at its worst."

"Yes, we were aware of it but only in so far as it impacted on our incident over in Elm Grove. Because of the accident, it took all of our resources longer to get to the scene. So forgive me if I don't have a full picture of what went on." replied Eddie.

"Ok, let's start at the beginning. Over the years we have built in a traffic system that allows traffic coming down from the sides of the valley to access the freeway in a safe manner. The link roads are spiraled to ensure that speed is reduced to an acceptable level and crash barriers are placed on all corners."

"Yes, I hate coming down those particular roads," Eddie sighed, "They are a pain in the neck."

"Pain in the neck they may be, but in the last seven years, since they were installed, we have never had an accident. That is up to now," said Bill.

"So what happened on Friday?" Maria asked.

"From what we have been able to establish, it appears that a black colored Prius, driven by the head psychiatrist in the hospital at the top of Raven Hill, The Minerva Psychiatric Rest Home, came down the hill at approximately six forty-five p.m. Somehow it jumped the third last barrier and careered on to the freeway where it was hit by an eighteen-wheeler, giving it no chance. The Prius was pushed onto the outward lane killing one other person. In the meantime, the truck jack-knifed, taking at least ten other vehicles with it."

"So what's not right Bill?" Eddie queried, "It all sounds very logical to me, so far."

"Well, if a car jumps on to the freeway, the outcome is classic. We have no problem with that. The question is why did Doctor Mitchum's car, by the way that was the doctor's name, jump the barrier? Remember that these barriers were designed to the highest specifications. To do that it is estimated that it would have to be travelling at a speed in excess of forty miles per hour. Now Doctor Mitchum has been driving down that road, on and off, for almost ten years, without a problem." said Bill.

"So that raises the question, did he have a heart attack or was the car faulty?"

"Precisely." said Bill. "However, the car and Doctor Mitchum were incinerated in the collision. Initial investigation seems to indicate that the first impact with the truck fractured the fuel line and the second impact on the outward lane ignited the spilled fuel and we had a proverbial fireball."

"Speculation is one thing, but without evidence you have zilch and from what you tell me, all you have is a mass of burnt-out metal." suggested Eddie.

"I know Eddie, but I have a feeling and it won't go away." said Bill. "I have spoken to his widow and she said that he was due home as they were due to go out to a show that evening. When she rang him to see where he was, she said he sounded bothered."

"Ok Bill, we will have a chat with Mrs Mitchum and see what she has to say," responded Eddie, "but you now owe me one! Will you call Doctor Mitchum's widow and ask her if it would suit for us to call on her in about one hour's time? Text me if there is a problem."

"Let's do it now," said Eddie, as they left the Traffic unit. "I hate this side of the job, talking to the bereaved. They must be going through hell. She is probably feeling guilty at ringing him and possibly putting him under pressure to get home in a hurry."

"I think we should visit the clinic first. Then see what the scene is like before we talk to the widow." suggested Maria.

"Good thinking. I still can't figure out how the car could have jumped the barrier." said Eddie.

Chapter 20

Fifteen minutes later they pulled into Raven Hill which was well hidden on the top of the hill and surrounded by a variety of hedges and shrubs. The road leading up to it was steep and winding with corrugated steel crash barriers evident on all of the turns. When they spotted the police tapes that marked the point where the car had left the road they stopped the car and got out to examine the scene.

"Bill mentioned that there were no signs of brake marks, therefore," mused Eddie, "the car must have been travelling fast and bounced off the left-hand rock face of the avenue and that bounce was enough to lift it over the barrier. That is my theory, what do you think?"

"It sounds reasonable, but it does beg the question – why was it travelling out of control? Was it a mechanical, a mental or a health problem?" Maria asked.

"Maybe it was just an accident after all." said Eddie, "While we are here let's see if we can have a chat with someone in the clinic. At least we should find out a little about Doctor Mitchum before we meet his widow as you suggested."

As they drove into the forecourt of the clinic, which was a single story building with what looked like Virginia creeper covering the entire façade of the building, they noted that on the right-hand curve of the forecourt there appeared to be a number of out-buildings.

Maria identified one of the signs indicating the laundry, another indicating store. On the left the driveway curved to the pillared portico of the main door. A solid oak door. Having identified themselves through the intercom, they were admitted to the lobby before being finally admitted through a second door into reception.

Unfortunately, the matron was at a meeting when they called but Miss Jane Starling, the assistant matron, invited them in and was only too willing to talk about the terrible tragedy that had hit the clinic. She was a slim, middle aged woman with a very quiet disposition, eager to please but with little or no authority. Her hair was a mousy brown tied back in a bun by a grey ribbon which reflected her personality or lack of it.

"Thank you for seeing us without an appointment," said Eddie, having introduced Maria and himself, "We were just in the vicinity, on our way to call on Mrs Mitchum, and just wanted to get some background on the doctor. What can you tell us about him?"

"He was such a lovely man. The patients adored him and the amount of good work that that man did for all his patients is immeasurable."

"How long has he worked here?" asked Maria.

"I would think about two to three years in his current position. However, prior to that he was employed as a consultant. He was very much in demand by a number of clinics and ours was just one of them. He did give that up when he became Senior Psychiatrist with us here, about three years ago."

"Would it be possible to see his office?" asked Eddie. "His certificates should give us some more information as to when and where he graduated from."

Doctor Mitchum's office was a picture of order. Every pen, paper, and paper clip was placed in neat order on his desk. No sign of disorder in Doctor Mitchum's life. On the wall were a number of certificates outlining his various and numerous qualifications. On the desk was a laptop computer – nothing else. A steel filing cabinet was placed in the corner.

"Is it alright if I take a copy of the certificates?" Eddie asked, as he prepared to photograph them with his cell phone.

"No problem at all. It saves writing down all the details, doesn't it?" said Miss Starling.

"Tell me, did you notice anything peculiar about Doctor Mitchum last Friday?" asked Maria, as Eddie took the photographs.

"Doctor Mitchum was a very quiet and gentle man, always the perfect gentleman." Miss Starling replied. "So I must say, I was surprised to see him almost running out to his car on Friday. At the time I didn't take much notice of it other than to notice that he was leaving later than usual. He was such a stickler for time. You could set your watch by when he came and when he left. He was ruled by his watch."

"Had he seen many patients on Friday? Or can you find out?" asked Eddie.

"Well, this clinic is unique in so far that while some patients are confined to the clinic by order of the court, it is a semi -open facility. In other words, in addition to the residential hospital section, a separate section is open to non-residents. In this clinic non-committed patient can be referred by their own doctors for assessment." said Jane Starling.

"So Doctor Mitchum could have had both types of clients on Friday? Is that what you are saying? To be specific, can you tell me what his schedule was for Friday evening? That might throw some light as to why he was late leaving." said Eddie.

"Sorry, but I have no access to his private diary. However, Matron Smyth would have full access to his clinic diary. I will get her to call you when she is free, if that is alright with you. I'm sure you appreciate the need for patient confidentiality."

Thanking Jane for all her help, they carefully drove down to join the freeway and headed to visit the doctor's widow. On the way they discussed what they had learned from their visit.

"Seems to have been quite a qualified guy," opined Maria. "Judging from the number of certificates on his wall, I counted twelve."

"Yes, his primary certificates were awarded by that college north of Wayward Creek, Charleston College." said Eddie, "With the more advanced psychiatry degrees being awarded through online study. At least that is how it appeared to me."

When they arrived at Doctor Mitchum's house, with the aid of their SatNav, they noticed how picture perfect it was with its brightly painted frontage and well-kept garden. Someone was obviously an ardent gardener.

"I bet this would be amazing during spring and summer. Even now it looks so colorful," said Maria.

"Hope we haven't kept you waiting," said Eddie as he introduced Maria and himself. "We were delayed over at the clinic."

"No problem at all, I really appreciate you taking the time to call. I realize you are so busy but I just don't know what to do." said Mrs Mitchum as she introduced herself as Beth. "How could such a thing happen to us? We never harmed anyone and this has destroyed our lives. Something must have gone wrong. Maybe they had the barriers in the wrong places. Or maybe his foot slipped on the brake. Oh my God, what are we going to do?" cried Beth.

"Yes, it is so hard to rationalise these things Mrs Mitchum." said Maria. "So many whys and so few answers. You must be devastated. Would you like me to get you a cup of coffee? Then we can talk all about it and see if we can put sense on any of it."

"You probably think I am either mad or over-reacting. When I look back at our lives over the past year or so, so many things don't seem to make sense. Tom and I have been married six years. Even though we have no kids, our life was so predictable and as Tom would say, so serene. He loved that expression. He always said that it expressed ultimate contentment," said Beth.

"So do you think that over the past two years Tom changed?" Maria suggested, "Was it pressure of work or what?"

"To be honest with you, I don't know," said Beth, "It is so hard to pin down. So many little things. For instance,

Tom was always an open book. I could predict everything he would do, or how he would react to certain things.

However as late as last week, I was coming back from the library, up past the university, it must have been last Friday week. You see Friday is my day for the library and I could have sworn that I saw Tom's car going up Market Street. His car is so old it would be hard not to recognize it.

Anyway, when he came home I asked him what he was doing up Market Street, as I had seen his car there. He got very defensive, saying that it was impossible to have seen it as he never left the clinic on that day."

"Did anything like that ever happen before then?" asked Maria.

"Yes, on two other occasions in the past, I thought I had seen his car in different places but I just didn't think too much about it. Until now."

"You mentioned that there were some other things that you thought were out of the normal."

"Yes, I have been looking back over the past few months, trying to make sense of it all. Maybe he was depressed or stressed from seeing all those patients. Who knows?

Anyway, we are a one car family and so, when Tom would come home, I would maybe go and do some shopping. He hated shopping. And on a few occasions I would feel that the seat position would be different. Tom and I had the same seat position always.

I remember that when I mentioned it he asked me was I getting paranoid. He said he had dropped a coin and had to move the seat to find it. Anytime it happened after that, I ignored it. Although I hated having to readjust the seat. He should have put it back properly, shouldn't he?" said Beth as she started crying again. "I also found some empty paper bags in the trunk on one occasion, they were from some sort of electronics shop. The type of shop I just know that Tom would have no reason to visit."

"How did he explain that?" asked Maria.

"I suppose I never asked him at the time. It is only now that I am looking for a reason as to why this has happened," said Beth.

"Did he ever talk, without mentioning names, of course, about any of his patients?" intervened Eddie.

"No, of course not. He was so strict about patient confidentiality that if he ever heard a colleague do so, he would get so annoyed."

"You must have known him so well. Can you tell us when and where you met him?" asked Maria.

"Believe it or not, we met at a high school dance in a little town. You may know it, Wayward Creek. I can still see him looking oh so serious but oh so dashing in his tux. It was love at first sight, for me and I do believe it was likewise for Tom. However, we had to wait, Tom's decision, until he had graduated from the local college in nearby Charlestown before getting married. Everything had to be right for me, he would say."

"So did Tom start working here immediately?" asked Eddie.

"Oh no, he had to serve his time in a few other clinics before getting the position of Senior Psychiatrist, here, about three years ago. We have been so lucky and so happy to be here, that is until now. I just know that something isn't right but I can't put my finger on it."

"Well Beth, if you think of anything else, please call us on this number," said Eddie, giving her his card, "In the meantime we will make some enquiries to see what we can find out."

"That poor woman is in a bad place," Maria commented, as they got back in the car. "It's bad enough to lose your partner but to have all these doubts now must be hell for her."

"She is obviously suffering from shock at the moment," said Eddie. "I think we should talk to her again in a few days' time. In the meantime, I would like a word or two with the matron. This time we will make an appointment."

Chapter 21

As they were exiting the driveway, Eddie's cell phone rang.

"Hi there, hope you have time to talk to a very important TV researcher who has just been tasked with finding out the true value of growing one's own vegetables! I joke you not, detective. That boss of mine is trying hard to send me to an early grave. Apparently the government is reacting, as usual, to the recent report from the World Health Organization (WHO) on the perceived epidemic of obesity in our children. So now I have to research the whole 'area of growing your own'." was Shirley's opening remark.

"Well actually my partner and I are heading back to the station right now. See you in the Costa Café across the street in thirty minutes for coffee and a sandwich? Its lunch time. Ok?" said Eddie.

"Wow! That sounds serious. Could that be the petite TV reporter you particularly don't like? Or is it you don't like particularly?" ribbed Maria.

"Oh nothing serious. That is indeed Shirley our TV insider. She is just looking for help. Remember it was she who gave us the steer on to Julie, who in turn led us to the diary. So you scratch my back and I'll scratch yours. ok?"

"I bet you would and probably did, scratch her back!" laughed Maria.

"Very funny," replied Eddie.

When they got back to the station, Eddie asked Maria to call the matron and make an appointment with her while he went to meet Shirley.

"So, are you now the newly appointed agricultural Correspondent?" joked Eddie, as soon as Shirley had joined him in the café.

"You might think that funny but I don't," replied Shirley. "I thought that I had eventually moved from that kind of assignment. But obviously not, in Butch's mind."

"What happened to your research into Gregg Newman's family?"

"My idea was to do a feature on the effect on, not just the victim's family life, but on the family of the accused. For instance, what would become of Newman's daughter if he was sent to prison? He has sole custody of her and nobody seems to know where her mother is. Even if we knew where she was, she has no say in her daughter's future. That can't be right."

"So just because you hit a stone wall Butch has cancelled that assignment, is that it?" asked Eddie.

"Well yes and no. I don't know where to go with the

story and I had to admit that to Butch. What else could he do but give me something to do! Hence the vegetable story. Big deal!"

"I think that I told you my father was a policeman and he always told me that when you come to a dead-end, go back to the beginning and retrace your steps. You will find the opening that you missed on your first assessment. Sometimes we get blinded by what looks obvious at first glance. Go back to the beginning. When Alice came to Oldtown, she got a job in the firm that Newman worked in, right?" said Eddie.

"Yes, but nobody seems to know where exactly she came from."

"She must have applied for the position, so they must have a record of her application. If you find that, you will find out her previous address and details of her qualifications and the college that awarded the certification. Start there and see where it brings you."

"Thanks Eddie. Now I feel like a proper idiot. Of course, I should have thought of that!" said Shirley "It's back to Oldtown for me, first thing tomorrow morning. Will you miss me?"

"I'm missing you already. Tell me more about your family. I think I need to know what I am getting into before it is too late!"

"Wow, you are getting serious, Mister Detective. Let me see where to start. Did I mention to you last night that my father is a mass murderer and that my mother keeps a brothel?" replied Shirley earnestly.

"No, but it's beginning to make sense. Which of these endearing characteristics did you inherit? Maybe I am as well off not knowing!"

"Seriously, my Mom and Dad were born and bred city folks and I was the one and only adored offspring. Both Mom and Dad worked in the local bank where they met and eventually married. Unfortunately, Dad died of a heart attack four years ago."

"I'm so sorry to hear that. It must have been a terrible shock to your Mom and you."

"Since then Mom lives on her own and insisted that I have my own life. So I moved out and got myself an apartment. Which, by the way, you have yet to visit."

"That was hard."

"Yes, it was hard to take at the time. He was only fifty-five years of age and looked the picture of health. Unfortunately, inside he was very worried and concerned at the direction the bank was taking. He always maintained that any fool can lend money. It is the wise one who ensures that it is repaid."

"Isn't it amazing the extent to which some people,

especially men, go to hide what is really bothering them?" Eddie mused.

"Eddie, I don't believe what I am hearing. You really have a soul! You old softie!" Shirley laughed.

"Enough of that. Care to see a movie tonight?" asked Eddie. "Much as I would like to chew the cud here with you all evening, I have a partner covering for me across at the station. I will call for you at seven thirty p.m., ok?" said Eddie, leaning over to give her a quick kiss.

"Great, I will look forward to that and in the meantime, I will research the cost of organic versus genetically modified vegetables. How exciting!"

Chapter 22

When Eddie got to his desk, Maria had already arranged an appointment with Matron Sue Smyth, at the clinic, for three thirty p.m.

"Hi Eddie, have you been over to Traffic?" asked the Chief, as he was passing by.

"Yeah, we had a chat with Bill and then called to the clinic. Unfortunately, the matron wasn't available then so we have an appointment with her at three thirty p.m. We also called to the widow of the guy from the clinic. She is in a bad state, which is understandable, trying to make sense of it all and grabbing at straws. She just feels that something is wrong but doesn't know what exactly that is."

"Good work, keep me posted. In the meantime, keep the team working on the Gregg Newman case. I hear that he is a very angry man at having to publicly withdraw from the election. According to McNally, he is, to use his words, 'going to aggressively defend his innocence'."

"I don't know how he is going to do that. The case is stacked against him. The pathologist's report states that, for the prong of the buckle to have ended up embedded in the victim's throat, a very considerable amount of force had to be applied, it could be assumed therefore that this was deliberate and not an accident. Plus, only Newman's and the victim's fingerprints were on the belt and I assume that she didn't strangle herself."

"He was never one to back off a challenge. This will be some challenge."

"The only way he can get out of this, in my view, is to plead that the act was consensual and that it was a case of accidental killing. But even if he tries to go down this road, we have him for statutory rape on at least one occasion. According to the victim's diary, assuming that it is allowed in court, this arrangement with the victim went on for almost a year. That means that when they started it, she was well under the legal age."

"Are you following up on that aspect of the case?" asked the Chief.

"Yes, we have contacted the parents of the two babysitters that Lucy Spinks told us about, for their permission to talk to both girls. Also I understand that five or six years ago, back in Oldtown, there was talk of Newman being accused by his wife, in public, of having sex with their then fifteen-year-old babysitter. At the moment this is only hearsay but we will follow it up."

"By the way, did you say that you had an appointment up in the clinic at three p.m.? Well you had better get going, it's almost three p.m. now." said the Chief.

"Thanks for reminding me, but the meeting is at three thirty p.m." said Eddie.

Matron Sue Smyth was the epitome of what a matron should look like. She was tall, slim and stern looking with steel rimmed glasses. Her whole bearing was one of competence and understanding of what the clinic's role was; the patient's welfare came first and last in her mind. Anything that took from or upset that objective was not acceptable. While she was prepared and indeed seemed to relish talking about the great work that the clinic did, she was not prepared to breach patient confidentiality, in any way. Having welcomed Eddie and Maria into her large office, she retreated behind her desk.

"What can I do for you today?" she began. "I believe my assistant gave you some information yesterday."

"Yes indeed," said Maria, "Miss Starling was most helpful, but we appreciate that she wouldn't have all the information that you have access to. For example, we are trying to uncover anything that might explain why Doctor Mitchum could have such a horrific accident on a well-protected road that he knew so well." said Maria.

"Doctor Mitchum was indeed a man of routine but that is not to say that he was rigid in his work routine." Matron replied. "He believed in getting his patients involved in practical things. He believed that the patients, by concentrating on external exercises such as yoga or painting or robotics, gained an enormous beneficial effect and hastened their recovery."

"That sounds like very advanced thinking, but can we just go back to his patients and his normal interaction with them. I assume he saw his patients in a professional manner in his office and kept a diary. I also understand that you can not divulge the names of his patients or if they were patients from the clinic or his personal non-clinic patients."

"Quite correct," said matron. "That information is sacrosanct. Regarding his interaction with the patients, he was very much 'hands on' and encouraged them to develop their own personal development ideas. For instance, it was one of his private clients who developed the yoga sessions which she also ran very successfully twice a week. The other patients and indeed people living locally loved the sessions."

"Can you tell me how many patients, Doctor Mitchum would see on any normal day and how many he saw on Friday last." asked Eddie.

"Well one of the reasons that Doctor Mitchum was so predictable was that he always worked to the hour. Every session with a patient lasted fifty minutes and each session commenced on the hour. So, he would commence at nine a.m. and complete four sessions by one p.m. He would take one hour for lunch and a walk around the gardens. Then he would have two more sessions up to four p.m. From four p.m. until six p.m. he would see his private patients, and we would have nothing to do with that." said matron pointedly.

"We appreciate the need for confidentiality, however on the basis of what you have told us, he should have been leaving here shortly after six p.m. Correct? And yet the accident didn't happen until six forty-five p.m.," Eddie reminded her. "Have you any idea what delayed him?"

"I must admit that I was not aware of the fact that he was obviously late leaving. It is most unlike him to vary from the norm," replied matron, "I will check the log and see if there was any kind of emergency with one of his patients and let you know if I find anything out of the ordinary."

"Thanks matron, we very much appreciate your help and we won't keep you very much longer. This probably was just an unfortunate accident where the traffic barriers just didn't do the work that they were designed to do. It is now back to the city engineers to check out why this happened."

"But why did it happen to Doctor Mitchum? He was

such a careful driver."

"Yes, that is the sixty-four thousand dollar question the answer to which we may never know." agreed Eddie. "Before we go, can you tell us a little about this facility? I have been aware of its existence for years now but I have never really understood its function."

"Well, without boring you, we have been in existence now for twenty-five years. We were set up as a 'halfway house' for State Patients – those are people committed by the law as insane. Now I'm sure you will appreciate that there are many and varied degrees of insanity. Some may never get cured, others react favorably to medicines and counselling and therapy. So, when patients show signs of improvement, in the high security facilities upstate, and to make room for new patients, a certain number of them are sent here to a less rigid security facility. Now that is not to say that patients here are free to do as they please. No, patients are monitored all day and every day."

"So if the courts find someone insane and commit them to a psychiatric facility, is it for life or can it be for a specific period and if so, how can one get release?" queried Eddie.

"Well now you are asking the hard questions. I hope you are not in a hurry as the answers to those questions could take a long time," replied matron.

"Maybe you could give a quick summary."

"Briefly, before a patient can be returned to society, he or she must show that the imbalanced behaviour that had them committed has been corrected. They may then apply to the court for release. That application has to be supported by two independent psychiatrists and a general practicing doctor," said matron.

"Thank you so much, matron. Again please accept our condolences on the death of your colleague and sorry for taking up so much of you time," apologized Eddie as both he and Maria got up to leave the office.

Chapter 23

"Those places give me the creeps," shuddered Maria, as they drove back to the station.

"Yeah, it's frightening to think of so many people locked up with so many shrinks. I would hate to be them!" Eddie agreed. "But seriously, what did you make of matron?"

"I got the impression that she wanted to protect the good name of the clinic and didn't really want to delve too deeply into Doctor Mitchum's death. A peculiar sort of reaction I would say."

"Yes, kind of cold creature with a smile. I'd like to analyze her!" Eddie joked. "Anyway there is little else we can do. No usable corpse or car wreckage to work on. No problem request from the clinic and the city engineers are closing rank on the safety of the barriers. Close the book and we will do our report and get back to wrapping up the Gregg Newman case. We have plenty of other problems to investigate without wasting more time on this," said Eddie.

"It is sad to think that what appears to be a good man, a good husband and a very good psychiatrist dies in such a simple way." sighed Maria. "For years he had been coming down that hill without a problem and then, not only does he kill himself but so many others as well. Life is so unpredictable."

"He will be sadly missed; I am sure by a lot of patients. Imagine all of his patients will have to start all over with a new shrink."

"I had read somewhere that in progressive clinics it was recommended that patients be exposed to things like art." Maria added, "Apparently it takes the focus away from them and concentrates the mind on a manual task. The article mentioned a number of successful artists that started their painting as part of their therapy."

"Well, as matron said, the yoga classes he introduced, as well as the art classes, were highly successful both in maintaining the physical health of his patients but also in calming them," Eddie reflected. "He will surely be missed."

"I know you think we should call it a day and finish off our report but I have been thinking, Doctor Mitchum was, by all accounts, a very disciplined and particular type of man, right? So he obviously would have been particular about his car. Especially having regard to its age. So, he surely kept records of any or all of the services the car got. If so, that information would be in his home and not in his office. Maybe we should call his wife and ask her." Maria suggested.

"Look Maria, I think we should not raise her hopes

of finding something sinister about the accident," Eddie retorted, "We are obviously up against a stone wall. Maybe he had the car serviced, maybe he didn't. Even if we did find something, it would not alter the fact that the body and the car were both incinerated. I say we leave it be."

Chapter 24

When they got back to the station there were messages from two of the babysitter's parents, wanting to know what was going on, and why the police wanted to talk to their teenage children.

"Ok Maria," said Eddie, "I think you would be better talking to them. They might find talking to a male officer a little more intimidating."

Twenty minutes later Maria called to Eddie. Both mothers had agreed to speak to them that evening. Luckily both lived adjacent to each other so it would be possible to fit both interviews in that evening. So much for the early night that Eddie had hoped for. He had better call Shirley and tell her that he might be late for the movie. What a start to their relationship.

"Let's call on Nora O'Connor first – it's the nearest. Then Amanda Cruz – she lives about a quarter of a mile further on."

The first thing that Eddie noticed as they pulled into the area where Nora O'Connor lived was how clean and well-kept it was. Even though it was in a less opulent part of the city, there was a distinct sense of pride in how the houses and the gardens were kept. The little church boasted not only the national flag but also the Irish tricolor. This was a very definite Irish part of the city.

"I will let you take the lead role in the interviews." said Eddie, as they pulled up outside the front door.

"Thank you for agreeing to talk to us Mrs Sullivan. My name is Maria Diego and this is my partner, Eddie McGrane," said Maria, as Mrs O'Connor met them at the door.

"Please come in and tell me what this is all about." Mrs O'Connor replied, as she led them into what appeared to be the 'good room'. Everything neat and shining. Plenty of family photographs on the sideboard and a crucifix hanging over it.

"This is my daughter Nora. She babysat for the Newman's on a few occasions." continued Mrs O'Connor, introducing a very shy and conservatively dressed young girl sitting on the couch.

"This won't take very long," said Maria. "I am sure you are aware of the tragic incident that occurred in Mr Newman's house last Friday evening. We are just making general enquiries from other girls who babysat for Mr Newman in the hope that they may have some kind of information that would help us understand what could have happened."

"Oh that poor girl. My heart bleeds for her and for her suffering parents. What is the world coming to?" said Mrs O'Connor. "Nora babysat for him on only a few occasions, as I mentioned, isn't that right Nora? She has Irish dancing classes on two nights a week. And that seemed to clash with the nights, particularly Friday nights, that Mr Newman wanted babysitters."

"Is it alright if I ask Nora a few questions?" asked Maria.

"Certainly," said Mrs O'Connor, "Anything we can do to help, we will."

"Maybe you could start by telling us how you came to babysit for Mr Newman. Who contacted you on the first occasion?" said Maria.

"There is this noticeboard up in our school," Nora replied, "and people put notices up on it for various things like 'waitresses wanted, books wanted or for sale' and now and again there would be a notice for someone wanted to babysit. Well, last year I answered one of these notices and rang the number on it."

"Can you remember who answered your call?"

"Yes, it was a man. He introduced himself and although I didn't know him, I recognized his name. When I got home I told my Mom and she knew of him as a well-known lawyer. He was very polite and friendly on the phone and agreed to give me the job."

"Did you discuss it with any of your school-buddies?"

"Yes, I did and I was surprised at the reaction of some. At the time I assumed that it was sour grapes on their part."

"What kind of comments were they making, Nora?"

"Well they would be making comments about sugar daddies and special pets and things like that. To be honest I had no idea what they were on about. It did however seem to give some of them something to laugh about," said Nora.

"So, on the occasions when you did babysit for Mr Newman, how did he treat you?"

"Oh, he was always very professional. The first time he got me to complete a job application form. Just for his records, he said. After that he was always so polite and caring and his rates were above what I would normally get elsewhere. On a few occasions he did give me a little extra. I think he saw me as an older daughter to Tracey. When I would be leaving he would help me on with my coat and give me a hug. He probably knew that my Dad had passed away last year and was being extra nice to me."

"Tell me Nora, would Mr Newman contact your home landline if he wanted you to babysit or would he call you on your cell phone?"

"Oh, he would always contact me on my cell phone. He would joke that I was old enough to make my own decisions."

"When Nora told me that, I felt it inappropriate behaviour on Mr Newman's part." Mrs O'Connor interjected. "After all Nora is only fifteen years old and wouldn't be used to that kind of attention and so we decided that Nora had enough other activities at that time in her life."

"So what happened the next time Mr Newman rang Nora?" asked Maria.

"I explained to him that I had Irish dancing classes on the particular night but he persisted and said he would change his arrangements if I could babysit on alternative Friday evenings. He got quite annoyed when I said I couldn't babysit for him again and hung up the phone on me. I didn't think he would be like that. He was always so charming."

"Have you heard of any of your school friends babysitting for him since then?" asked Maria.

"Yes, there have been a few other girls from the class ahead of me who babysat for him. The talk was always of how well he treated them. Money seemed to be no problem. Many of the girls would be seen sporting nice new outfits and even one girl was supposed to have got a new cell phone."

"Thank you so much for your time Mrs O'Connor, and a special thanks to you Nora. It's not easy talking to police. If you think of anything else, please contact us at this number." Maria said, handing Mrs O'Connor her contact card. "Also, if you can think of the names of any of those girls you mentioned. We would very much appreciate it."

Chapter 25

As they drove off to visit the second babysitter, Amanda Cruz, Eddie said, "Well, what did you make of that? It seems to me that Mrs O'Connor smelt a rat in the grass, at an early stage."

"Yes, she was lucky that Nora was the innocent type of daughter that discussed everything with her mother. Otherwise I think Newman might have had plans for her."

Even though the Cruz house was within a quarter of a mile from the O'Connor house, it was like moving into a different world. Most of the houses seemed to be in disrepair and none of them seemed to have been painted for many a year.

Mrs Cruz met them at the front door but made no effort to bring them inside but moved a few of the many items on the front veranda to make room for them to sit on dilapidated chairs. There was no sign of her daughter.

Having introduced themselves, and shown Mrs Cruz their IDs, Mrs Cruz said in a very defensive voice, "My daughter is a very good girl and never did anything wrong. No matter what Mr Newman might have told you. Anything she got, Mr Newman gave her. She never once took nothing that was not given her."

"Did Mr Newman tell you that Amanda had taken something that did not belong to her?" asked Eddie.

"Yes, he did on one occasion. I noticed that Amanda was wearing a very expensive bracelet last Christmas. When I asked her where she got it she said that Mr Newman had given it to her as a Christmas present. I didn't believe her and rang Mr Newman. He denied giving her any such thing and that she must have taken it by mistake and not to worry. He would sort it all out with her. She obviously gave it back as I never saw her wearing it again."

"Did Amanda say anything more about it to you?" asked Maria.

"You know what young teenagers are like. They tell you what they think you want to hear and no more. Ever since our divorce she spends more time with her father than with me and her younger sisters. She thinks she is too grown up for them. God help her. She is only a child, sixteen years of age and thinks she knows it all."

"Did she ever discuss Mr Newman with you?" asked Maria.

"She started babysitting for him when she was about fourteen years old and at that time we had a reasonable relationship. She would tell me a lot of what was going on with school, friends, and all that kind of thing.

I remember her telling me how nice Mr Newman was and how well he was coping since his wife left him all alone with his young daughter. I also remember that he paid well and Amanda would always give me some of her earnings. She was very good to me at that time as she was aware of how it was for me since Sam had left me."

"So, if everything was as good as that, why did Amanda stop babysitting for him?" asked Maria.

"Well, Amanda was always a grade A student and all of a sudden her grades began to drop and she seemed to become a different kind of child. Aggressive and what I called self-opinionated. She would argue with her sisters and with me over the smallest thing. I felt that she was doing too much babysitting and that those sessions were becoming later and later. Now, on those occasions Mr Newman would always get her a taxi."

"I wonder would it be possible for us to speak to Amanda, Mrs Cruz?" asked Maria.

"I don't know if she could tell you any more than I have."

"Sometimes, Mrs Cruz, we find that by hearing another person telling the same story we find one small nugget that helps us to understand something." Said Maria, "So if it is all right with you we would really like to speak with her."

If Nora O'Connor was the epitome of conservativeness and innocence, Amanda Cruz was the very opposite. Her whole appearance was that of a twenty plus rather than a sixteen-year-old girl. Her attitude to her mother's request to speak to the police officers was one of defiance, as she strutted onto the veranda.

"Thanks for seeing us Amanda." began Maria. "We really won't take up much of your time. Your mother has filled us in on the main facts that we needed. But tell me a little about Mr Newman. What kind of a man was he to work for?"

"He was a lovely man to work for and respected me, listened to my opinions. Not like other people who think you are still a child. If my teachers had minded their own business, I would still be working for him," said Amanda, "wouldn't I?"

"And if that would have been the case, Angie Lummox would be alive today. Did you ever think of that?" asked Maria.

"Oh God, no! No, I suppose I didn't think of that but I do know Mr Newman well enough," Amanda replied aggressively, "to know that those rumours are rotten lies. Mr Newman would never tie a girl up."

"Well, Amanda, as you say, they are only rumours and that is what we are trying to do, dispel such rumours.

So I'm sure it is fair to say that he never suggested tying you up at any time."

"Of course not, he was always so gentle and caring. He would never have even thought of hurting me. He always said that I was special for him." said Amanda.

"Yes, it sounds like he really liked you Amanda. Do you think he even loved you?" asked Maria.

"Of course he did. He told me every time."

"He must have been very lonely, with his wife having run out on him. Did he ever talk to you about that?"

"Of course he did. We talked about everything. I told you he treated me like a woman, not like a child."

"So it was natural then for him to want to make love with you. Was it a big decision for you to do that the first time?"

"You don't answer that Amanda. They have no right to ask you those kinds of questions!" interjected Mrs Cruz.

"No. It was the most natural thing in the world. He was so understanding and gentle and made me feel all grown up, as he said it would," continued Amanda.

"Amanda, we must warn you that the age of consent in this state is eighteen. You have admitted having had sex with Mr Newman and this may be used in court, when you may be served with a subpoena to attend. I would ask you to think carefully before answering my next question. Did

Mr Newman coerce you in any way to have sex with him?"

A very different Amanda now sat with her face in her hands having realized what she had said and the implications for both her and for Mr Newman.

"It all started so nicely. He would help me on with my coat and hug me and sometimes his hands would touch me accidentally and he would apologize. Later on he kissed me and that led to other things. He did warn me that if I ever told anyone, he would see to it that my mother would be evicted from this house. When I stopped babysitting for him he made me swear not to tell anyone about what we were doing. Oh my God, please don't send me to jail!" Amanda sobbed.

"Amanda, you won't be going to jail," said Maria, "but we do need you to come down to the station tomorrow and make a full and detailed statement. Also we would ask you to think of any other babysitter you know of, who babysat for Mr Newman and who might have a similar story to tell. Mrs Cruz we would like you to attend with your daughter. Does ten thirty a.m. suit you both?"

"Yes, we will be there." said a very subdued Mrs Cruz.

Chapter 26

"Sorry I had to take a rain check for tonight Shirley," said Eddie when he eventually got her on her cell phone. "Maybe we should try being pen pals! It probably would be easier to manage."

"No problem Eddie, I know exactly how it happens. I'm back down to Oldtown in the morning, thanks to your brilliant advice, Mister Detective. So how about we try again on Thursday evening?" said Shirley.

"Perfect. It's dinner, followed by a show on Thursday evening, even if half of the city gets murdered or robbed. I'm off duty. Take care in Oldtown and the best of luck chasing the elusive Mrs Alice Newman." said Eddie.

Wednesday morning dawned wet and windy. Not just rain, but horizontal rain, rain trying to get in through any weakness in the house and according to the forecast there wasn't any sign of a let up during the day. Not the ideal weather for a two-hour drive to Oldtown, thought Shirley, as she set off on her journey. Her boss, Butch, had reluctantly agreed to her spending one more day on what he called her wild goose chase. On the other hand, he wanted her report on the pros and cons of organic foods on his desk by Friday. No pressure!

Once she got onto the freeway, traffic eased somewhat and she made good time and arrived at the Chronicle's office by eight thirty only to find it still closed. They obviously didn't keep city hours of business.

While she was waiting, Shirley thought of getting herself a coffee but with the rain still showing no sign of restraint, and the probability that the coffee shop, like everything else in the town, didn't open early on a wet day. She decided to spend the time in planning the rest of her day. She was aware that the law firm that Alice and Gregg Newman had worked in was now run down and run by a distant cousin of Newman. Whether they would have retained employee records beyond the statute of limitations was the first thing to explore. She hoped Don at the Chronicle would be able to help her on this.

In the meantime, she began to try and analyzes her feelings for Eddie. What was it, she wondered, that attracted her to him from the very first time she saw him at Newman's house. What had passed between them on that occasion? He did have a sense of purpose about him but only in a quiet and relaxed kind of way. When he had spoken, his voice was definite but respectful – not like so many who, just because they were police officers, seemed to exude a powerful arrogance.

On the two occasions they had been together socially,

she didn't really class them as dates, she had an immediate sense of feeling good and comfortable with him. He had no airs or graces about him. Just good manners and she got the feeling that he was content in himself and was very happy in his work, which he took very seriously. Did she see this as a plus or as a minus? Already he had to cancel their date due to his work, so yes, she admitted it was a date! Would this be a pattern? Only time would tell. On the other hand, her kind of boyfriend and now ex-boyfriend, Jeff, had a very casual attitude to work. He didn't particularly like the concept of doing it every day.

Looking back on her 'love life' she really had only one long term relationship. That was with Mark Cauldron whom she met in her final year at college. It lasted almost two years. The fact that they had even talked about marriage now sent a shiver through her body. How did she get it so wrong? Their relationship ended eighteen months ago when a mutual friend told her that, not only had he gambled away all of his own money but was up to his neck in debt all over the city. Of course it also riled her to know that her mother's constant doubts about him had been confirmed.

So could she now be wrong about Eddie? But that was a ridiculous question to ask herself. She didn't know him, so how could she be making these decisions and assumptions? Just go with the flow and enjoy getting to know him. If something good came out of it, so be it. So why did she have butterflies in her stomach, just thinking about him and looking forward already to tomorrow evening for their first proper date?

Before she could tie herself further in analytic knots, there was a knock on the window.

"Have you been here all night?" said Don, "Down here, as you will find out, when you get sense and come and work for us, we don't start work until roughly nine a.m. Depending on the weather and other things, like the time of year. Come on in and I'll see if Matilda has the coffee brewing. By the way, her search, according to her, was unsuccessful. No records could be found in our archives."

When they were seated in Don's office with mugs of steaming coffee in their hands, Shirley said, "Don, you're a treasure and I appreciate all that you have done for me, but, work here in Oldtown – no, not on the cards, I think I am in love and the object of that love is back in the city. However, if that falls through I may just hide here in your office."

"Well now I know where I stand in your affections, a sad second. Tell me what I can do for you today." said Don.

"Don, I have one more day to prove to Butch that I have a story to tell. If I can track down Newman's wife. I really feel that while the public focus is on the perpetrator and the victim, nobody seems to realize the impact that the crime has on both families. For instance, if Newman is found guilty and gets a custodial sentence, who will look after his eight-year-old daughter Tracey? Is his ex-wife entitled to regain custody? These and many other questions have to be asked and solutions found. I want to interview Alice Newman and see what she has to say about these questions."

"You sure are on a crusade," said Don, "So what can we do?"

"Eddie, that's the light of my life, is a detective who by a coincidence is working on the Newman case. He has suggested that I go back to the beginning and find out who Alice is and where did she come from?"

"That makes good common sense to me."

"He suggested that I go to the firm they both had worked for here in Oldtown and see if I could get a look at their HR records. That should give me details of her qualifications and where she graduated from. That in turn could lead me to her home town and family. If she has such a thing!"

"If I was superstitious I would say that the cards seem be very carefully stacked against you. The law firm that Newman worked for here in Oldtown was Newman and Stuart. The Newman part of the partnership was

Newman's grandfather and on his death his father took over and bought out old Dee Stuart who was glad to get out of a declining business. At that time most folks here were beginning to hire the up and coming law firms who had moved to the city."

"So who runs the firm now?"

"The firm, if you could call it that, is run by a distant cousin of Newman's. Her name is Faith Newman, a seventy-year-old lady with a tongue like a razor but she has a kind heart! She operates from a one room office over the local book store looking after basic legal matters. Now as regards records, well like ourselves, as I already mentioned to you previously, we didn't have the resources to invest in a proper archival system. Well neither did she and so when the original office, in Broad Street, went up in flames two years ago, I believe, so did a lot of records."

"Well Don, I'm not superstitious but I don't believe in coincidences, something is not right here. It looks like someone is making it difficult to find Alice and that makes me all the more determined to find her but I am running out of time – I can hear Butch screaming already."

"Well let's stop wasting time and go and visit the lovely Faith and see what she has to say. Let me warn you – she may be feeble looking but don't let that fool you – she is as sharp as a blade and could eat you raw and spit out the bones!"

Luckily the rain had eased off and the walk to Newman's office only took five minutes. Whatever hope Shirley had in her mind of making progress soon evaporated as she climbed the well-worn stairs to the office of Faith Newman, Law Clerk. The office itself was small and every single inch of it was covered with files that seemed to be just scattered and abandoned where they had been placed or just opened. Obviously the filing rooms that had suffered in the fire had never been refurbished. Behind the battered desk sat Faith smoking a thin black cheroot.

"If it isn't my good friend Don Harding, the intrepid reporter in search of a good story." said Faith "And who is the beautiful young assistant you have with you today? By the way Don, if you are looking for legal advice on a divorce, take my advice, she is too young for you. Now young lady, I am Faith Newman, and who are you?"

"What a wonderful reception," laughed Don. "You never change, you old rascal. As usual I am looking for free information. My friend here is Shirley Green from the big city. She is researching a story on victims of crime and is anxious to contact Newman's wife Alice but no one seems to know where she is. We were hoping that you might have salvaged some of your staff records that might lead us to where she came from."

"As far as records are concerned, my dear, forget about

it." Faith replied, while puffing smoke in all directions, "Absolutely nothing survived the blaze. Regarding Alice Newman, I did always wonder where she went to. Before we knew what happened, Newman was up in the city and the marriage was kaput. Very strange and very sudden. She seemed to be a lovely girl – much too good for our Newman, if you ask me."

"Well it was worth a try anyway," said Shirley. "Thank you for seeing us. If you think of anything here is my card, you might call me."

"Hold on a minute," said Faith "there might be someone who can help. Just wait while I make a phone call."

"Hi Sue, Faith here. Just a quick call. Do you remember my cousin Gregg's wife Alice? You do? Good. Can you remember where she came from or anything about her? It's important?"

Five minutes later she relayed the information she had received.

"Sue was a young clerk who worked in the office about the time that Alice arrived and would have been her age group. She vaguely remembers Alice saying that she graduated from a place called Wayward College or something like that. The name struck her as peculiar for a college. Unless it was for wayward kids."

As they were walking back to Don's office, Shirley was already Googling 'Wayward College' but could find nothing. They were back to square one again.

Chapter 27

At nine a.m. on Wednesday morning, Chief Ned Brennan and the DA, Mary Donnelly together with Eddie and Maria were seated around the table in the incident room.

"Ok Eddie, where are we at now?" asked the Chief. "Any further developments?"

"Let's start with Newman," began Eddie.

"One. He admitted having arranged to meet the victim in his house with a view to having sex. He would deactivate the alarm on his lunchtime jog and text Angie to advise her of the time to be there later that evening. She knew where the keys to the back entrances were.

Two. He admitted that it was a regular arrangement but says his sex life is his own business as he is an adult and not married and Angie was also single.

Three. There is no evidence of unidentified fingerprints in the room. That is except for the victim's prints, which we have now recorded.

Four. The tape from the hidden camera clearly shows him having sex with the victim. But it looks likely that the recording is of two different occasions and there is no recording of the evening in question. Very strange. The prints on the camera are his and only his.

However, I find one small issue that I am not completely happy with. The video stops each time before he leaves the bed so it doesn't show what happened next. Now maybe it was set to stop or someone else stopped it. I wonder…" said Eddie.

"But if there are no other prints, how could that be?" asked the DA.

"If we look at it from Newman's defense, it is a possibility that someone, someone very clever, set it up and wiped the camera clean. I think we need to be very clear on this," said Eddie.

"Let's now look at the pathologist's report," Eddie resumed.

"The victim was asphyxiated by a leather belt being placed over her head and around her neck. The belt was then tightened manually until the victim was dead. There is no disputing this.

It would have taken a lot of strength to do this. The results show that the victim, although tied to the bed, did struggle against the ligature."

The victim had a small amount of alcohol in her blood together with some sort of sedative."

"So are you happy with the pathologists report?" queried the Chief.

"Yes, I think that is very conclusive," said Eddie.

"There may be a question as to how Newman, given his condition, could have had the strength to do it. But I don't think that is likely to be questioned."

"On the other hand the Toxicologist's report is very interesting," continued Eddie. "It showed that the level of alcohol in Newman's system far exceeded what he claims to have drunk. He admitted to having three whiskeys with his staff and that is verified. He then stated that he was forced to have a 'tumbler of whiskey' by the intruder. Added to that we analyzed the tablets we found by his bedside and they are a combination of pain killers, sedatives, antidepressants, pick-me-uppers and let-me-downers. You name it, he had them all. Now most of these are available on prescription only. So where did he get them? The report shows that he had consumed a mixture of these drugs with the alcohol."

"Have you checked with his doctor?" asked the DA.

"Yes, and he states that he never prescribed these drugs for Newman and as a matter of fact Newman had a problem with pill popping, as he used to refer to it," said Maria. "We then checked the pharmacies adjacent to Newman's work and home and all say that these are tablets used mainly in hospitals only and that they did not stock them except for special prescriptions."

"So where did the drugs come from? Can we prove

that they were his? Once again his and only his prints were on the container but he denies knowing anything about them." said Eddie, "To date, our enquiries indicate that they are the types of prescriptions that hospitals specialize in, but that is in no way conclusive, as yet."

"I think we need to tighten up on a few of these points. By the way, well done to both of you, apart from these loose ends, it is looking good to go," the DA added.

"Thanks," said Eddie. "Our team have put a lot of work into this. However, I would like to review the charge against Newman. He has been charged with accidental killing on the basis that death took place while doing a legal act. It now appears that he was committing an offence by having sex with a minor. We now are led to believe that this is not the first time he has committed this offence. At least two other babysitters are considering giving evidence against him. Furthermore, we have reason to believe that the reason for his divorce was that his wife had accused him of sleeping with their then babysitter."

"Have you had any report back from the Oldtown police?" interrupted the Chief.

"The police in Oldtown are following that up for us but so far they have been unable to locate the young woman. It is understood that she had left the state some years past. However, leaving that aside for the moment, I believe we now need to change the charge to involuntary manslaughter," replied Eddie.

"Yes, I fully agree with that. This will certainly change the playing field." said the DA.

Wait until the press get a hold of this. So far, apart from NTTV and a few of the tabloid press, the broadsheet press coverage has been very mute. That shows you the power his Party has over the press but that can only last while there is no new and scandalous information coming out. In the light of what you are saying, we will have to go public on the new charge so we can't keep the lid on it for much longer." The Chief suggested.

"Before we go any further," Eddie intervened, "we had better get statements from the two other babysitters. And also check with our colleagues in Oldtown and see if they had any luck in trying to locate the babysitter who was responsible for the row that Alice had with Newman that led to her disappearance. Once we have those signed statements we should then advise Newman's attorney of the position. We owe him that courtesy and it is not going to affect the outcome of the case.

The Party have already jettisoned Newman, and are looking at damage limitation. Claiming that his withdrawal from the election was health related. They will probably lean on us to hold off on the charge until after the election but that's two weeks away and I don't think we can hold off that long."

"No, we are not going to be led by them. We are going to press on regardless but we do need to have everything nailed down firmly. Whatever happens now, Newman is finished in this town!" The Chief commented. "The Party have disowned him, the proposed partnership in the firm has been cancelled and as a matter of fact, I have it from a good source that he will be looking for a new job, even if he is acquitted. Which he won't be."

"The thing that amazes me," said the DA, "is the way that he continues to deny everything. He emphatically denies tying the girl to the bed and strangling her. In spite of the irrefutable evidence to the contrary."

"Is it possible that he is telling the truth?" asked the Chief.

"The evidence we have would contradict that possibility. I would think that his mind is totally confused due to the effect that the cocktail of drink and drugs he had in his system has had on his brain." The DA replied.

Chapter 28

The rain never let up all the way back from Oldtown and even listening to her favorite music on the car radio couldn't lift Shirley's spirits. She had run out of time and Butch's patience. She figured that she could cobble together a story on victims but that would lack impact if not tied together with a high profile case like that of Gregg Newman.

Up to now the station had managed to keep the story alive, in spite of threats from advertisers to withdraw their business. However Butch wasn't for turning and the more abuse he got, the more he was determined to pursue the story. He was aware of the two-sided sword that reporters had to balance in being close to political parties. In many instances it was a case of 'you don't scratch my back and I won't scratch yours!' None of the other investigative reporters were able to come up with something new but he hoped that Shirley, with her uninhibited enthusiasm and youthful good looks, might get the break they needed.

Now that hope was gone and Shirley was in no doubt where her next assignment would be. She would need Eddie's support more than ever now.

"Hi Eddie," she spoke to his voicemail, "On my way back from a wet and miserable Oldtown with my tail tucked firmly between my legs. The final doors have been firmly closed against me and feeling very sorry for myself. Call me when you get the chance."

'Oh God, I hate leaving phone messages. I sound like a pleading schoolgirl,' she thought as she hung up her hands-free phone.

About thirty minutes later she spotted a roadside café and rest rooms and pulled in. She had just been served her coffee when her cell phone rang. "Shirley Green, I told you I was not ready for marriage – yet." jibed Eddie. "Now, what has happened to dim your beautiful positive outlook on life?"

"Oh nothing much! Just hit another stone wall and can't see my way around it. Now I have no doubt that someone with your intelligence and experience would have no problem in finding the solution. Help me please!"

Ten minutes later when Shirley final took time to take breath. That is when she had recounted to Eddie the story of her unsuccessful trip to Oldtown, she just said "Please help."

"Let's look at this rationally," said Eddie. "The first thing you must realize is that the courts have dissolved their marriage and taken Tracey and all responsibility for her and given it to Newman. Alice is now a free agent and may be anywhere in the world if she wants to be."

"But what about Tracey's life? Surely she is entitled to the care and protection of her natural mother if and when Newman ends up behind bars?"

"Unfortunately, the answer is no. If Newman ends up in jail he can nominate a carer for her. That's the law, honey. Crazy as it seems. Now, I will pick you up as agreed at seven o'clock tomorrow evening, for dinner and a film, ok?" Eddie confirmed. "Just jot down what you have found so far and I will have a look at it and see if I can unlock the door. Sometimes the obvious is staring us in the face."

Just as he hung up the phone Maria walked in to his office. "You have interesting visitors waiting to see you. Gregg Newman and his attorney, Al Mc Nally, would like a word with you."

"Wow, you had better send them in, and Maria, you stay also. I don't trust that pair."

"Thanks for seeing us without an appointment, detective," began Al McNally, as they were all seated. "Gregg is very anxious to make sure that his statement is being fully investigated. He is adamant that someone else was in the house that day, unbelievable as it may seem."

Once again, Eddie was taken by the change in

Newman's demeanor, gone was the flamboyant exterior and the immaculately dressed 'male model'. In its place was a very aggressive and worried Gregg Newman.

"Well, I can assure you that every shred of evidence is being fully and impartially followed up on, Mr McNally. We have checked and double-checked every inch of the house and there is no evidence whatsoever of a third party being there. But have no doubt, if there is the slightest shred of evidence, we will find it. We checked on your Taser and yes, it was in the floor safe with your fingerprints on it. I assume you are the only one with the combination to that safe, Mr Newman?" asked Eddie.

"None of this makes sense," said Newman, "I know the smell of my wife's perfume was everywhere in the room and I noticed it on other occasions also. How do you explain that detective?"

"I'm sure you will agree that it would not be unusual for young girls of your daughter's age to mess around with their mother's cosmetics; especially if she is not around to see them. Perhaps that would be an explanation? The only smell we got was that of whiskey." said Eddie "And speaking of your wife, or should I say, ex-wife, can you tell me where she is now?"

"The whereabouts of Mr Newman's ex-wife is of no concern in this case, detective." replied Al McNally.

"That is precisely what we believe also. It was Mr Newman who brought up the subject, as you are well aware. He can't have it both ways. He either believes he is telling the truth, in which case we may need to talk to her. Otherwise she is of no concern in this investigation."

Without warning, McNally jumped up and excusing them both, ushered Newman out of the office.

As soon as they got into his car, a now furious Al turned to Gregg and said, "You have any idea what you nearly did in there? Do you realize that by bringing up the subject of your wife that you are opening up a door for the police to investigate her whereabouts?"

Thirty minutes later they were seated in ex-judge Leo Forrest's study where Al outlined what had happened at the police station.

"You actually claimed that your wife was at your home and not only that, but that she was responsible for your actions!" said an unbelieving Leo. "Let me remind you of the facts Gregg. Your wife came between you and your political ambitions. And you couldn't handle it. That night when she appeared in the Country Club and attacked you, it was like a gift from heaven to us. I'm sure you remember it well."

"Of course I remember it, I'm not that stupid!" snapped Gregg.

"Well then, stop acting stupid for once in your life!" retorted Leo. "We used her outburst that night as an excuse to solve your problem. Yes, we, and that includes you, arranged at a private court sitting under the late Judge T.M.Wilson, to have your very difficult wife declared insane and, under an assumed name, committed to a private clinic. You didn't want to know where she was going just as long as she was out of your hair. You didn't even want to know anything about the arrangements. We, Teddy Moran and I, had to make the financial arrangements and we, Teddy Al and I, had to source a doctor to take care of the medical side of things. We did all that to protect your political career. Did you ever stop to think what would happen if any of this became public?"

"I can appreciate how you must be feeling," said Al, "but we can't have the press nosing around. Already NTTV are scratching around Oldtown and interviewing friends of your ex-wife. Luckily it is a very small station and we have the newspapers in our pockets – up to now. Forget about your wife. She is gone. But don't forget that if the truth ever gets out, you and every one of us, who solved your problem that night could end up in jail. Is that clear, Gregg?"

"That's all fine and dandy for the Party but what about me?" Gregg scoffed. "I'm about to be stitched up for something I didn't do!"

"Listen Gregg, you blew your future when you, once again, let down your trousers and the Party. Now, with a good attorney and a bit of luck, the murder or whatever it is going to be called, can be contested as a consensual act gone wrong. God alone knows how the 'sex with a minor' will go. You made your choice. Now you have to pay the price." Leo snarled.

"Remember Gregg, that everything you do between now and the case coming to court, is being watched. If you believe there was someone else in your house that day and that they set you up, prove it. The police have stated that there was not a shred of evidence to say otherwise." Al added.

"Between now and election day, you need to be seen publicly endorsing Erin for mayor. Once we have achieved that we have more power to help you. And no more talk about your wife, ok?"

Chapter 29

"What do you make of it all, Maria?" asked Eddie, when McNally and Newman had left his office.

"It looks like the lady spoke up once too often and in the process was airbrushed out of the operation to have Newman elected." Maria surmised. "She was just an appendage to the handsome Newman and went and spoilt his party and paid the price."

"But where is she now and why did McNally cut off any discussion on her whereabouts? There is a story there somewhere."

"Sure looks like it. If only we had the time to look into it. What was her maiden name?"

"I think, from memory, that it was Alice Mason, or maybe Masone, but I am not sure. Why do you ask?"

"My son likes to think of himself as a' techy 'and would enjoy spending his time trying to trace someone like this. I might get him to have a look when he is finished his homework. It's amazing what these young ones can find even if they can't find their own socks." Maria laughed.

"Good idea, come on and let's get some lunch before something else happens. Coffee and a sandwich is on me." said Eddie.

As they were seated in the café across the road from the station, Eddie commented, "You know Maria, we have been partners for almost a year now and today is the first time you mentioned your son. I suppose that is because I never asked. I don't tend to mix work with personal things as it may complicate relationships, particularly in our kind of business. Tell me about him."

"Well, he is fourteen years old and wants to be a policeman like his mother. His father wants him to develop some 'way-out' software system that he can sell on and become a millionaire and pay off the mortgage on our house. Simple as that!" laughed Maria. "But he is a good boy and has managed so far to keep out of trouble."

"Lucky you." said Eddie. "We never got around to having kids. I suppose I was too focused in catching the bad guys and it became my only way of life. Jenny didn't see it that way and I think we were really incompatible from the start and every time we tried to fix a leak, another one emerged just as quickly. We lasted just two years."

"Sorry to hear that." said Maria. "I don't suppose there has been anyone else since then, has there?"

"No. I'm still trying to catch the bad guys. My father was the same, except that my Mom felt the same way and always seemed to be there with him."

"So what about that little TV girl? You know the one

you can't seem to remember!" Maria reminded him.

"Now that's the problem, she seems to be different. I think." said Eddie, "But it's very early days. Wait until she gets to know me!"

"Don't be too hard on yourself Eddie. And, for God's sake, give her a chance before you decide that she doesn't like you."

"Thanks for listening to me. It beats going up to the shrinks on the hill to be analyzed," said Eddie. "Now it's time to get back to work and earn our pay."

"You know Eddie, ever since we visited that clinic I have had bad dreams about what those people do to the minds of poor people who can't handle some crises in their lives. Does it ever bother you to think that you could be pumped full of drugs just to calm you down?"

Chapter 30

When Eddie said seven o'clock he meant seven o'clock and so at precisely seven o'clock he was standing outside Shirley's door. His right hand on the door bell, his left hand behind his back.

"Is this the residence of that well-known TV personality?" he called, as Shirley opened the door.

"If you mean the one that does the agricultural reports, then you got it in one," came Shirley's reply "and what has the gentleman got behind his back. Pray tell me?"

With that, Eddie produced a multi-colored bunch of roses from behind his back and very casually handed them to her.

"The local park was open as I was coming up here and I just picked these. They appeared to be growing wild there!" he joked.

"Thanks Eddie, you old softie. Hold on while I put them in water." Shirley giggled.

That set the scene for the rest of the night. As with the previous night, they seemed to be oblivious to the rest of the diners around them and almost missed the time for the film. A film neither could tell the name of the following day.

"By the way, did you jot down Mrs Newman details," asked Eddie, during a break in the meal.

"Oh yes I have them here," said Shirley as she produced the note from her purse. "Let's hope you can do something with them. I would just love to prove Butch wrong. I have given him more breakthroughs than any of the other reporters but he is never satisfied. He knows I have nowhere else to go and keeps pushing and threatening me with the agricultural portfolio even though he knows that I know zilch about that."

When they got back to Shirley's apartment later that night, Shirley again invited Eddie in for coffee. This time he said yes. However, when Shirley brought in the coffee, Eddie said,

"Shirley, I want to be totally honest with you. I like you too much to want to hurt you in any way and while I would just love to jump into bed with you right now, I want to be really sure before I commit to anything that important to me. So, can we take it nice and easy and see where it brings us?"

"That's perfect with me, Eddie. I know you are just out of your divorce and the easy thing to do is jump into the first relationship that comes along. But I know you are not like that. Just be with me please – I need you." Shirley whispered. The next two hours were spent cuddled together on the couch watching the Late Show.

Chapter 31

As Shirley was about to sit down at her desk the following morning, Butch called her to come into his office. "Just a word Shirley. Well done with that interview last evening. You are really improving with each outing. Now the police have been on to us and want to talk to you about it. They have also 'requested' a copy of the full interview. Remember to keep your notes, they are yours and are confidential." said Butch.

"Thanks," said Shirley, "Mrs Brown did not ask that anything she told me be kept confidential."

"Good. Now I don't suppose you were able to locate said Alice Newman, were you?" said Butch.

"No, it looks like another stone wall but I will keep on trying." said Shirley.

"Look Shirley, that's enough searching. Time to draw a line under it and get back to the tasks I gave you."

No sooner had she returned to her desk and was once again about to sip her now lukewarm coffee than her phone rang.

"Hi Shirley, and before you get any notions, no I am not stalking you." said Eddie.

"Well, I am very disappointed to hear that detective and what, if anything, can I do for you this beautiful morning?" Shirley purred.

"Ask not what you can do for me but what I can do for you. I think one of our presidents had a saying like that. Anyway, you once mentioned that you didn't believe in coincidences, right?"

"Yep! That's me. I'm full of sayings, as you probably know by now."

"Well fasten your safety belt and tell me what you make of this. In the first instance the elusive Mrs Alice Newman, in her maiden state was known as Becky A Mason. In the second instance she graduated from a college upstate called Charleston College. It's near Wayward Creek. Now here is the interesting part or coincidence. Who else graduated from Charleston College? Only the late Doctor Tom Mitchum, the head psychiatrist from the Minerva Psychiatric Unit who was killed in that horrific crash on the freeway last Friday evening. Now tell me, is that a coincidence or what?"

"Wow, are you sure? I mean how did you find that out?" replied a shocked Shirley.

"I can't talk to you right now but if you are around at lunchtime maybe we could grab a sandwich and coffee across the road and I will fill you in on what we found out."

"Ah Eddie, that's not fair! Don't keep me in suspense."

"Sorry, Babe, got to go." said Eddie as he hung up the phone.

"Just the break I need," thought Shirley as she headed back to Butch's office to tell him that she had another 'lead'.

"Hi Chief," said Eddie as he entered the Chief's office, "this is probably nothing but I think you should know. Newman's wife Alice was christened Becky A Mason. She obviously dropped the Becky bit, not too flattering for an ambitious young woman, and took her middle name, Alice, when she applied for the job in Oldtown. Nothing wrong with that either. The interesting part is that she graduated from Charlestown College, upstate.

Again nothing wrong with that. However, this is where it gets interesting. When Maria and I visited the Raven Hill Clinic, we had a look around the late Doctor Tom Mitchum's office and noticed that according to the certificates that adorned the wall of his office. He also graduated from the same college. Coincidence?" Eddie wondered.

"Coincidence? Yes, but that's about it." the Chief replied. "Thousands of students will have graduated from Charlestown in the past ten years. It is a very good college with an excellent reputation. Now as far as I know, we have no issue with Newman's wife. She has been out of his life for years now and we are not looking for anyone else in this case. We have an open and shut case against Newman. Keep it that way. Don't muddy the waters with speculation. Newman would just love us to do that."

"Yes, I agree with you Chief, but it might prove necessary to talk to her at some stage and right now we have no idea where she is. Can I suggest that we put a request out to all clinics in the state asking if they have either Alice Newman or a Becky Mason registered with them?" asked Eddie.

"OK I don't suppose it can do any harm but keep it under your hat." the Chief warned.

All morning long Shirley was like a cat on a hot tin roof. She couldn't wait to meet Eddie and find out how he had found out about Alice. At one o'clock she was sitting at a corner table from where she had a good view of the station door. "Eddie please don't keep me in any further suspense! Tell me all about it!" she blurted as Eddie entered the coffee shop.

"Ok, ok, take it easy," said Eddie as she gave him a hug and a kiss, forgetting where they were, right in front of his colleagues.

"Maria, my partner, has a son who is a bit of a computer geek, or so she says. Anyway I was telling her about your efforts to locate Newman's ex-wife and she offered to ask him to use his know-how to trace her. Which he did. The fact that she changed her name when she came to work in Oldtown, using her middle name Alice, which was more sophisticated than Becky, made it a little more difficult to trace her using the methods that most people, including you, would have used."

"So now we know where she went to college and the name she would be known by. Now tell me about Doctor Mitchum and where does he fit in?"

"Well this is pure coincidence, and nothing more, as my Chief pointed out to me very forcibly. I happened to note, when Maria and I were in his office, that his certificates were from the same college. Coincidence? Not according to my Chief. He rightly pointed out that there must be thousands of graduates from that particular college working all over the state. Furthermore, Doctor Mitchum studied psychiatry, Alice Mason studied law. Two distinctly different faculties. Furthermore, look at their ages, there must be at least five years' difference which would make it very unlikely that they were in the college at the same time," said Eddie, "and finally and most importantly of all, my boss tells me to butt out and not confuse the case we are working on."

"Oh Eddie, I'm sorry if I left you in the 'you know what.' Thanks a million. You just leave Alice-Becky to me. I'm heading for Charlestown in the morning. By the way, how do I get there?" said Shirley.

"Shirley I will refrain from making sexist remarks as to directions and where females originate from! Of course I will drive you there. Isn't that what you were really saying?" said Eddie. "I'll tell the boss I'm taking one of the many days holidays I am due. It's under three hundred miles of freeway driving so we should leave here as early as possible and that will give us a long enough day to explore Charlestown College. It can't be very big."

"Oh Eddie, you are so understanding," Shirley purred. "I really believe that I will have very little trouble in house-training you. In the meantime, I will seek, with all of my skill, to win the Pulitzer Prize for investigative journalism. What time will we depart at? Better still, why don't you call here at say seven thirty a.m. and I will have breakfast ready and we could leave at eight o'clock. How does that sound, Mister Detective?"

"How in God's name did I ever get myself into this mess?" said Eddie, "I must be either mad and, by the way if I am, I am not going up to that clinic, or just mad about you! I think I will go with the latter. Yes, seven thirty sounds perfect and remember I like my eggs sunny side up!"

"Now Eddie, my Mom always advised me to start as I intended to finish. Who said anything about eggs, sunny side up or otherwise? I was thinking more of a cup of coffee and if you were lucky, a slice of toast! See you at seven thirty," laughed Shirley.

Chapter 32

"Hey Eddie, a lady to see you!" the Station Sergeant shouted to Eddie, as he headed for the water cooler.

"Oh good morning, matron," said Eddie, when he recognizes Matron Sue Smyth from the clinic. "Come on in and have a seat and tell me what I can do for you."

"Well, I am sure you will appreciate that we are still trying to come to terms with the terrible tragedy that happened just a week ago today," said matron.

"Yes, I can fully appreciate how you must be feeling at losing a colleague and such an invaluable one at that. Have you found a replacement for him yet?" asked Eddie.

"Replacing him is going to be almost impossible. He had so much experience and he bonded so well with even the most difficult of clients. However, we must regroup and look after our clients to the best of our ability. They are the ones that count," replied matron.

"Indeed, they are the ones who must be most vulnerable. How are they reacting to the news?" said Eddie.

"As can be expected, with deep shock, some more so than others." said matron. "However, while my main reason for calling this morning was in relation to permits for our upcoming annual fundraising event, I thought it opportune to ascertain from you if it is alright for the clinic to hand over Doctor Mitchum's personal items to his widow. I realize that the interment is to be tomorrow. We will be meeting up with her and I would like to know what to say to her in this regard."

"Thank you for asking matron, but I see no reason whatsoever as to why you should hold on to any of his personal belongings. The Traffic Corps have submitted their report and I believe the verdict was accidental death due to either mechanical failure in relation to the vehicle, or blackout on the part of the driver. Apparently Doctor Mitchum was having his blood pressure monitored over the previous few weeks, something his wife was not aware of."

"Yes, I myself was unaware of that," said matron. "He did always seem to be so much in control of his health. He always gave the impression that nothing could faze him. I am however reminded of the adage 'still waters run deep'. Maybe he carried too much unshared stress."

"Yes indeed. One never knows what another person is carrying on their back," said Eddie.

"However we now need to carry on and prepare the office for whoever takes his place. The advertisement is ready to go in the press early next week once the interment is over." said matron.

"Just one thing matron, if you wouldn't mind. Could you take an inventory of his belongings and perhaps give both his widow and us a copy?" Eddie enquired. He wasn't quite sure why he made that request. Old habits die slowly.

"I will certainly do that, detective. By the way I read that letter you sent to all of the clinics looking for a Mrs Alice Newman or Becky Mason. Well I can confirm that we don't and never had a person of that name registered with us. We will, of course, be replying formally today."

Chapter 33

The first thing Eddie noticed, as soon as Shirley opened the door, was the smell of bacon and eggs.

"Ok let's go," said Eddie, as he turned on his heels as if to go.

"Don't you dare," said Shirley grabbing him by the arm. "I have spent the last hour, well maybe that's an exaggeration, trying to get the eggs sunny side up for you. And hungry or not, you are going to eat them, Mister Detective!"

Being Saturday, traffic was very light and as a result they were on the freeway shortly after eight o'clock and headed north. Just over three hours later, most of which time Eddie listened to Shirley recall her early childhood and aspirations, Eddie felt that he had begun to understand what issues and beliefs drove her to be what she was, a very unique young lady. To her, religion was a way of living, not just rituals and while she held firm to her beliefs, she admired others who held firmly to theirs. As their SatNav told them to pull in to Charlestown College, Shirley said, "It was your turn to listen on the way up here. It will be mine on the way home!"

Having negotiated the town of Charlestown with the aid of their SatNav and having arrived at the college, the first thing that struck both of them was the size of the campus. Both had expected to find a small nondescript college in the middle of nowhere.

In fact, it was a huge modern looking combination of granite buildings set on the side of a hill and surrounded by acres of forests. Trees that were now in all their autumnal glorious colors of orange red, brown and yellow. An amazing sight. The college itself was buzzing with activity, even though it was a Saturday.

It must have catered for two or three thousand students. While the granite faced buildings were impressive, the grounds, with their running tracks and football pitches and facilities seemed to stretch for miles around the building.

Shirley had phoned the previous day and had made an appointment to meet the college administrator, a Mr Ike Bolton, who was only too willing to show off the college.

Not wanting to interfere with Shirley's interview, Eddie excused himself and wandered around the facilities. He did however bring Shirley's camera with him with a view to taking photos of the college from interesting viewpoints just in case they might be of interest to Shirley, when doing her report on their visit, if it ever came to that.

"Well, Miss Green," said Mr Bolton, as he escorted Shirley into his book-cluttered office, "you mentioned that you were interested in one of our past students, Miss Becky Mason. I have retrieved her file and I must say that I immediately remembered her once I opened the file. She was one of those rare students who left a lasting impression without being, what shall I say, a stand-out." said Mr ('call me Ike') Bolton.

"What do you mean exactly by a not 'stand-out' type of person?" asked Shirley.

"Well some students are good, and know it, and show it off in a brash kind of way," said Ike, "Becky was the quiet well-focused kind, who didn't let flattery or anything like that get in the way of her studies. She graduated 'Summa cum Laude' in a very difficult faculty, law but to talk to her you would never get a hint of that."

"Did she have any close friends that you were aware of?" asked Shirley. "I am sure that someone with her looks and with her obvious intelligence would have been the desire of many a red blooded college student. Did she have any serious romances that you were aware of?"

"Well the reason I remember her at all is because she was very friendly with my own daughter who was the same age as her. They were both good students and helped each other with their projects. From time to time Becky would visit Heather, my daughter, at our house."

"So you must know of any serious attachments, wouldn't you?" asked Shirley.

"Oh yes, there were one or two, but from what I heard they were always on her terms. I don't however recall hearing of any very serious attachment while she was with us. I can't speak for what happened when she left. Normally the college would have kept in touch with her for a number of years after her graduation but eventually we lost contact. I think at that time she had moved to a new law firm. I may be wrong but I got the impression that she had met someone special. As both of her parents were by then deceased, she needed someone special to attach to," said Ike. "Enough of me rambling on. Tell me all about her? Where is she now?"

"I would love to be able to do that Ike, but the reason we are here is to try and find that out for ourselves. She seems to have disappeared out of sight. She was married to a Gregg Newman and had one child, but unfortunately the marriage didn't last too long. They were divorced about five or six years ago and she hasn't been seen since." said Shirley.

"Oh, I am so sorry to hear that. Unfortunately, she didn't join the Alumni and as a result, we would have no way of keeping up with her changes of addresses. However,

I will make enquiries from the other lecturers and if I find out anything, I will contact you." said Ike.

"Thanks, Ike. You see her ex-husband, Mr Newman, has been charged with an offence and we are covering the human aspects of the case, such as how it impinges on his family." said Shirley.

Chapter 34

As they were heading out the door, Shirley paused. "It seems a bit of a coincidence, but then maybe it is not, when I see the size of this college. We also came across another of your past students who was involved in an accident last week, Tom Mitchum. He was a psychiatrist in a clinic called the Minerva Clinic, up on Raven Hill in the city. We reckon he would have been here in the college some years before Becky was here."

"Tom Mitchum? That name rings a bell in this ding-dong head of mine. Now why is that? Let me see, that would have had to be in old Steven Hurst's Faculty. He was Dean of the Psychiatry Faculty for as long as I can remember. He has retired at last, but won't leave the building. He comes in every day and just wanders around looking for someone to talk to, or should I say to listen to him. A right pain in the ass, if you ask me. By a coincidence I noticed his car in the parking lot as we passed by. He has a tendency to park across two parking places and unfortunately one of them is invariably my one," said Mark, "You hold on here, while I see if I can contact him."

While she was waiting for Ike to come back, she texted Eddie to come back and take some shots of Ike's office and of Shirley interviewing Ike.

"Well, my dear, we are in luck, doddering Steven Hurst was actually looking for someone to talk to or maybe more accurately, as I mentioned, to listen to him, and would be delighted to join us," said Ike.

"That would be super," said Shirley. "I hope you won't mind but I asked my colleague to come in and take a few photos for my article."

As if on cue, both Eddie and Steven Hurst arrived in the office which was now very overcrowded.

"Hold on there while I fetch two more chairs. This office was never meant for conferences. I think it holds only just enough air for one slow breathing individual," Ike said with a chuckle.

"So, young lady. I understand from Ike that you have an interest in psychiatry. Wonderful. You know it is the most interesting of all of the faculties we have here in Charlestown." began Steven, settling comfortably into the only armchair in the office.

"No, Steven," Ike corrected him, "this young lady is doing research into the effects of crime on the victims of crime. She is following the history of one of our past students – someone you wouldn't know. However, you may be able to recall a student of yours. I can't recall his name, but you may remember he turned out to be an outstanding clinical psychiatrist and published a few highly acclaimed publications, if my memory serves me right."

"His name is Mitchum." chirped Shirley.

"Oh you mean Tom Mitchum. Oh yes. He is a world renowned psychiatrist. But what has he to do with crime?" asked Steven.

"My dear Steven, he has nothing to do with it, or should not, but these people have mentioned that he was in an accident last week and just wanted to know a bit more about him." said Ike.

"Oh, yes indeed. Is he alright? I am so sorry to hear that he had an accident. So many bad drivers on the roads these days. They should all be banned, if you ask me."

"And starting with you," muttered Ike under his breath.

"I remember him well," continued Tom, "always sends me a Christmas card every Christmas. He never forgets me. You know, he could have had a job anywhere in the world, with a mind like his. What a genuine human being. I seem to remember that as part of his Post Grad studies he would work in the Haven Private Clinic over in Broadway and one or two other nearby clinics," said Steven.

"How long did he stay in the Haven?" asked Shirley.
"Well he was only gaining practical experience while

studying for his doctorate. However, it was around that time that he came to me for advice. As I mentioned, he was a man with a conscience and was not afraid to stand up for his principles." said Steven. "I recall that it was the issue of 'committals' that got under his skin. He wanted the state law in this matter changed and asked for my advice and support, which of course I gave him. Not that it carried much weight with the morons up in the state administrative offices."

"So he didn't have much success?" asked Shirley.

"Well yes and no," said Steven, warming to the story. "If my memory serves me right, he identified ten cases where he felt there were questions to be asked regarding the court confinement and the ongoing support for these people."

"What happened to them?" asked Shirley.

"He did succeed up to a point in so far that he did manage to have the question raised at the Governor's office, who promised to 'look into it' and is probably 'still looking into it', without knowing what it is! As you will appreciate, in many of these cases the people requesting the committal didn't want the cases ever to be reviewed. The 'patient' was now out of their way and the last thing they wanted was someone looking for a review. However, he did have one piece of success. Apparently his attention was originally brought to this issue when he discovered a patient who had no known relatives, who had been declared insane and committed some years previous. She was still there about four years later and at no time had she had a judicial review."

"Would that be a common occurrence?" asked Shirley.

"Not so much now but in the past, unscrupulous families with the collusion of family doctors and legal people used it as a way of getting 'difficult' relations put away," said Steven. "The case in question was very interesting in so far that only the actual committal order was in the file in the clinic but without any supporting documentation. The order was signed by a judge who apparently was by then deceased and the court in which he presided at the time has no record whatsoever of the committal."

"But surely there had to be a record somewhere?" pleaded Shirley.

"You would think so, but, young lady, the law and those who control it, can be devious at times. As a result, Tom could not contest the order as there was no way of finding out what court had issued it. Anyway that didn't stop him and he eventually petitioned the Broadway court to have the patient transferred into his care at a clinic nearer to him on the basis that he undertook to look after her until a resolution could be found. I think that in order to keep Tom quiet, and to brush a very explosive incident under the carpet, the court agreed to his petition. I understand she was transferred as a private patient to a clinic where Tom had some involvement as a consultant psychiatrist, the name of which eludes me unfortunately." said Steven. "I think it had something to do with World War Two – the SS or something like that. Don't ask me what it is. The mind isn't what it used to be."

"Have you any idea of the patient's name?" asked Shirley.

"No, no my memory isn't what it used to be and of course, confidentiality in these issues is always so important. During the petitioning she would probably have been referred to as X or Y or some such identifiers," said Steven. "Now tell me how my friend Tom is? I hope the accident was a minor one."

"Unfortunately Tom was involved in a horrific car crash in the city. Both Tom and his car were completely wiped out. I am so sorry to be the one to tell you this awful news."

"What terrible news!" said a much shaken Steven. "What a waste of such potential. I never could understand why he chose to work in a backwater town like that. He should have been sharing his talent in the very biggest of our universities in New York or Washington."

Chapter 35

Having said their goodbyes and thanked both Ike and Steven for seeing them and giving them such valuable background information on both Alice and Tom they were driving down the avenue when Shirley said "Coincidence? Is that what you said? Coincidence my ass! This whole thing is beginning to stink to high heavens, agreed?"

"Don't jump to any conclusions. Yet." Eddie cautioned. "Right now we only have the remembrances of one, if not two, doddering old academics. As someone once said of academics, if they could do what they teach they wouldn't be academics. Anyway, I'm starving, let's find somewhere to eat and we can better review what we have learned today."

Before they left Charlestown they grabbed a quick meal in typical student type restaurant on the edge of town. Then it was on to the freeway and down south and home. Of course they had never stopped talking. As Eddie had said, "You can't just stop thinking about a system that can treat people like that. What kind of person would commit a relative to a life behind walls?"

For Shirley it was the scoop of her career. Wait until Butch heard of what she had uncovered. It was straight out of a crime novel. Evil men conspire to have relatives committed to psychiatric facilities, for life, state colludes in cover up. What a scoop!

"Easy on, Shirley. Before you start making public statements like that you must corroborate your facts and getting one doddering academic to agree with another doddery academic isn't sufficient corroboration to base an expose on. You will need to dig much deeper," said Eddie.

"Ok Mister Detective, you are right, as usual. God I hate when you are like that. Can't you be wrong – just for once?" Shirley teased. "So what do you think we should do?"

"Well in the first instance we are not going to do anything Babe," said Eddie. "You had better come up with a plan that will get you a list of patients in the Haven Clinic six years ago. It was around that time that Alice was divorced. Then you need to get a list of patients at all the other clinics in the state. I wish you luck with that. Remember what Stephen said about confidentiality? When you get that you should find a way in to interview the relevant matrons or better still the administrators. In the meantime, I am going to see if what we discovered will have any material effect on our case against Newman. I must be impartial in this, otherwise I stand to prejudice the case before it even starts."

"Sorry Eddie, it's been just me me me. Of course the case is the most important issue. But believe me, honey, I think I am on the cusp of making my name at NTTV and it's thanks to you, my Darling. You know that ever since I met you, my life has taken off at speed. I have never in my whole life been so happy and content."

Two hours later, having devoured an amazingly good steak meal, with Shirley cuddled up in the passenger seat and promising to stop talking and go to sleep, Eddie swung the car back on to the Highway.

Chapter 36

Two weeks later, Erin Sullivan was elected the city's woman mayor. It had been a hard fought election and it was by the smallest of margins that she beat Mark Swanson. The opposition had thrown every bit of mud that they had at the Democratic Party, especially focusing on the quality of the original candidate whom they continued to identify as being charged with murder and statutory rape. However, with the local press in their pockets, the Party capitalized on the fact that Erin Sullivan's background was squeaky clean and she had the backing of not only the female vote but of the ethnic Irish vote also. Gregg Newman was soon forgotten, yesterday's man. Well almost. Under the circumstances as Mark Reilly, Gregg Newman's boss, had put it: "It would be in the firms' interest if Gregg took time out until after his trial."

Very soon, Gregg Newman found that his many 'friends' were extremely busy and hadn't time for either coffee or lunch. In the Country Club he was someone not to be seen socializing with. He was even excluded from Erin's celebratory dinner, something he complained to Leo about, to no avail. Leo was also 'very busy'.

For the next two months, Joe Breslin became his

main companion as they worked on his defense. Joe was hopeful. His research to date had produced a number of witnesses who had recalled, under prompting from Joe, to seeing a strange car. It could be a Ford Taurus or maybe a Prius, in the vicinity of Elm Grove on a number of days in the past few months. Some others had thought they had seen someone, dressed in black with a black baseball cap, in the laneway behind the house. Joe was working on making these possibles become actuals.

In the meantime, NTTV continued to keep the story alive by regurgitating the facts as already known and by presenting a variety of interviews that Shirley had done with people in Oldtown who remembered the Newman's when they had lived there. Shirley also reported on the interview that she had done with Ike Bolton, the administrator in Charlestown College. This one had earned her surprise praise from Butch who then kept her busy with a number of specialist items, some still of an agricultural nature!

By this time Eddie and Shirley were an item, according to Maria, and met every chance they could get. She still had hopes of cracking the Mrs Newman mystery and pestered Eddie for ways and means to achieve it. (In the meantime, her mother was quietly planning what she would wear to the wedding.)

Chapter 37

Two months later, the trial of the State versus Mr Gregg Newman in the case of the death of Miss Angie Lummox began and lasted for four weeks. In the end it took the jury of seven male and five female members only three hours to arrive at a unanimous verdict on the charge of involuntary manslaughter – not guilty. And on the charge of statutory rape – guilty.

The judge, having thanked the jury, sentenced Newman to three years' penal servitude. As Newman was being escorted down to the holding cell, Shirley, who had been tasked by Butch to cover the case for NTTV, said to Eddie. "Well, that's one hell of a surprise, what do you think?"

"There is an old saying – the law is an ass. And I must admit, I can't reconcile the facts with the verdict." said Eddie.

Later that evening Eddie and Shirley were in their usual place in Nemo's, enjoying a celebratory dinner, just to mark the end of the case for both of them. By now Shirley considered herself to be the voice of NTTV regarding the case. She was there at the very beginning and now was there for the entire case and the sentencing of Gregg Newman.

"The fact that the trial took only four weeks, surprised me." said Shirley, "Of course the fact that Joe Breslin managed to challenge the credibility of the victims' diary knocked a huge hole in the prosecution's case. How did he get away with that?"

"From the beginning we had a doubt about that, but with Julie's corroboration we felt we were on solid enough ground. However once again Joe pulled a winger on us by casting doubt on Julie's evidence; insofar as she couldn't prove that even if Angie had shown her the diary, she couldn't prove that she had actually seen Angie writing up the diary. Very clever defense, just enough to throw the jury."

"I was sure and certain that the finger prints on the belt that strangled her would have been conclusive, yet that piece of evidence was seemingly ignored." Shirley mused.

"Not ignored exactly but once Joe had put doubts in the minds of the jurors, he was halfway there. Of course he had admitted that the belt belonged to Newman, so of course his prints would be all over it. That didn't prove that he had deliberately killed her, especially if the jury were now beginning to accept Joe's suggestion that there was sufficient proof that there was a third party involved."

"How did he get away with that?" Shirley wondered. "The evidence was clear that the police had questioned everyone in the neighborhood and checked the CCTV footages that were available and yet he was able to produce a number of witnesses who claimed that they had seen a suspicious car in the vicinity on a number of Fridays prior to Angie's death. He was also able to produce two neighbors who swore that they had seen a man, dressed completely in black, wearing a black baseball cap, on at least four occasions in the previous month."

"Joe always has the advantage, Shirley. As far as we were concerned we were just looking for information and asking if people had seen anything unusual around the date in question. Now Joe, on the other hand, knowing our position was putting it to people that they must have seen a strange car or van in the area, anytime during the past month. Similarly, he put it to them that there may have been a person in the area possibly dressed in black and of course, with a bit of prompting, some said that they did and even robust cross-examination couldn't budge them."

"Well at least there was no way out for him in relation to the statutory rape charge, in spite of his pleading that he thought Angie was at least nineteen years of age. The file he kept in his safe contained the job applications for all of his babysitters and each noted the girl's date of birth."

"Yes, that really nailed him," Eddie recalled. "If he hadn't insisted on showing us where he kept his Taser gun, we would never have found that vital piece of evidence," Eddie recalled.

Later on, having finished their meal and as they sipped their coffee, Shirley asked, "Do you really think he was guilty of Angie's death, Eddie?"

"Funny you should ask that. All the evidence we gathered says 'yes'. However, today I have an itch that I can't scratch. I'm not even sure where the itch is. Maybe when I wake up in the morning it will come to me. In the meantime, the Chief is pleased that we closed the case and justice, to a degree, is seen to be done. Newman is finished in this town. What a come down in such a short time!"

Chapter 38

"Hi Eddie, a call for you on line two. Another one of your young lady friends, no doubt. Why do they all want Eddie McGrane?" shouted the desk Sergeant.

"They must have seen you, that's why," responded Eddie.

"Hello detective, this is Beth Mitchum. I wonder if you could call to see me sometime if you can spare the time?"

"Certainly." replied Eddie. "When would suit you?"

"Well, I'm free tomorrow afternoon, if that would be alright with you?"

"Great, let's say two thirty, me and my partner Maria will be there."

The following afternoon, as Eddie and Maria headed out to visit Beth Mitchum, the snow that had been falling steadily for the previous twenty-four hours, driven by a strong north easterly wind that had swept across the lake, eventually began to ease off. While the snow ploughs had done their best to keep the main traffic routes open, the road leading into Mrs Mitchum's house, which was north of the lake, was treacherous, and it took all of Eddie's skill to get there in one piece.

"Thank you so much for coming out to see me, especially in this awful weather. You see I never replaced the car after the accident as I would be too nervous to drive after what happened to Tom," said Beth. "Would you like coffee? It just might warm you up. The weather is so unpredictable nowadays I never remember having so much snow this late in January."

Before very long she had a tray of steaming coffee and some cookies set on the table by the fire. Eddie and Maria were, by now, beginning to feel the heat of the fire and to perspire in their overcoats.

"So what did you want to ask us?" Eddie queried.

"I suppose I should start by saying that I have never accepted the version of events that led to Tom's death," began Beth, "and so, as I am sure you will appreciate, I have been examining every aspect of the accident and the time leading up to it, in my mind."

"Yes, that is quite natural," Maria agreed.

"Well, when the clinic eventually returned all of Tom's private belongings I just dumped them in the garage with the intention of going through them when I was up to it. However, a few weeks ago my bank manager called me in to discuss our joint account and I was stunned at the number of entries that I had absolutely no knowledge of. You see Tom always looked after our finances."

"That must have been very difficult for you," said Maria.

"Yes it was indeed. You see, I found a few debits that I had no explanation for, so I promised the manager that I would go home and have a look at Tom's files. It was then that I found the file on Taser guns. It had so much information in relation to their availability, instructions as to how to use them and the cost of them. When I saw this I realized that the cost of one these guns was almost exactly the amount of one of the unusual debits in our account. Then, as if I wasn't worried enough, I remembered that I had seen on the TV a few weeks back that the man, the politician, who was on trial for murder had claimed that someone had used a Taser on him. Of course my first fear was that somehow Tom was involved in all of this. Why would he want to know all about Taser guns? Was it just a coincidence?"

"Why indeed?" said Maria.

Seeing that what had started out being a quick chat, a cup of coffee and a little bit of reassurance for the widow was by now looking more likely to be a long session, Eddie asked if it would be alright if they took off their winter coats, as by now the perspiration was flowing down his face.

"Oh I'm so sorry! I should have realized that you are

kitted out for the weather outside and not for coffee in front of a log fire." said Beth.

When they were settled back a little further from the fire, Eddie continued, "Tell us more about the Taser gun and, if possible, can we see it?"

"No, unfortunately it was not with the personal items that the clinic returned to me," said Beth. "I went through everything, and it is not in that lot anyway. It was only when I was checking the unusual debits in his bank account that I found more entries that I had no knowledge of. As I delved further into the mess of files that the clinic had dumped on my door step I found that last year he had purchased the Taser on eBay, with a delivery address at the clinic. Now it is possible that he was acting for someone else but if so, there is no record of him being repaid. Now isn't that strange?"

"Yes, it is definitely very strange." Eddie agreed. "But let me reassure you, your husband was with a client during the period when the young girl was killed and we have him on CCTV running from the clinic to his car at six forty p.m., just before he had the accident. So you have no cause for worry in that regard. However, we do need to examine his movements and behaviour around this time."

"Certainly," said Beth. "Anything that would explain these debits would be a relief to me. Apart from the Taser thing, there were a number of debits in lady's shops and a rather large one from an electronics shop. Also there were withdrawals from ATM machines that were so far away from where Tom normally withdrew cash. It just doesn't make any sense to me."

"Ok," said Eddie, "what you now need to do is to list all of these debits. Exactly where and when they were made. Then you can see if you have any acceptable reason for them. After all he could have been buying items for you, surprise gifts for special occasions, for example."

"Oh no, not Tom! He was not that type of man. He would always ask me to buy something for myself on those occasions, especially if it entailed visiting a lady's shop."

"Well, as I said, Tom could not have been at the Newman's house on the day in question, so have no fears in that regard and anyway, as you know, the case is now closed. Regarding the bank items, I would suggest that you list the unusual items and by going through all of the files that were returned, try to reconcile them to possible purchases. If there is anything unusual about any of them that don't make sense, give us a call and we will have a look at what you find. Especially if you find anything that relates to a Taser gun." said Eddie.

Once they were out of the house and had put on their

coats and hats and were now trying to figure out how to get the car out of the snow that had drifted around it while they were inside, Eddie wondered aloud. "Something is not right here but I don't know what it is. However, if we get involved, the Chief will have our badges. This is obviously a domestic issue, the fact that it drifts across our recent murder case may be just a coincidence, if we were to believe in coincidences."

"If you go back to our original interview with Beth," said Maria, "we had her saying that she thought she had seen his car in various places that she could not explain. Tom was in the clinic on all of those occasions, as far as Beth was concerned. Maybe, without the Chief's blessings, it would be worth plotting where she thought she had seen the car and the dates and relate them to the shops in question and the location of the cash withdrawals."

"Do you want to go back to Traffic?" Asked Eddie, "because if you attempt to go down that road, and the Chief finds out, that at best, is where you will end up. Now let's just leave it with Beth and if she does find out something that needs our investigation, we go to the Chief and do it by the book. Now you sit in while I get the shovel and see if we can get the car moving out of this snow."

On the way back to the station Maria said, "I understand what you are saying Eddie, but I can't help thinking that there is more to the late Tom Mitchum than meets the eye. You remember when, on the Chief's instruction, we had the chat about the accident with Bill Johnson in Traffic? Well I would now, in the light of what Beth has said, suggest that we have another chat, and in particular, have another look at the CCTV videos that they had of that day."

"God, you are like dog with a bone - you never let go! Now what was it about the CCTV videos that didn't catch your eye then but now needs reviewing?" Eddie challenged her.

"I honestly don't know what it is but at the time we were just basically agreeing with Traffic that it was an accident and confirming that it was Doctor Mitchum that was driving the car. We were not looking for anything unusual or sinister. Now I am not so sure," Maria replied.

"OK, here's what we will do. When we get back to the station I will have a word with the Chief and suggest that we follow up on his original instruction and have a further chat with Traffic. If he says ok, then we have another look." said Eddie.

Chapter 39

Later on that evening, having had a pleasant meal in Nemo's, Eddie and Shirley were enjoying a quiet drink in Shirley's apartment. Shirley posed a question, "Eddie, we have been going out with each other now for a few months, so how come you haven't invited me to your place yet?"

"I suppose the simple answer is that I love it here. Your place is so warm and welcoming. The more complex answer might be that since my divorce, I have neglected to change things in my place. I'm sure you will appreciate that I have yet to exorcise the shadows of my ex-wife's influence on the place. I suppose it has become a bachelor pad in the meantime, with a lot of hidden shadows. It has however been my plan, as soon as I get time, to have the whole apartment redecorated. I don't suppose you would be interested in giving an opinion or even a bit of advice on how I should go about it?"

"If that's your idea of a wedding proposal, Eddie – go take a running jump for yourself!"

"There you go again, I'm talking of change and immediately that equates to marriage in your mind! It reminds me of the couple who were thirty years married. She said 'You're not half the man I married'. To which he replied, 'Of course not – you have spent thirty years changing me!" laughed Eddie.

"Seriously, I would love to give an input. When can I start?"

"Let me get rid of a few things first and then I will give you the tour. I will then look forward to hearing your suggestions. Now tell me the latest news from Butch? Has he yet realized the absolute gem he has working for him?"

"Butch is Butch and he is never going to change as far as I can see. In fairness to him, ever since I covered the Newman trial, he has taken me off agricultural events and promoted me to more human interest issues and I love it."

"That reminds me," said Eddie. "Do you remember the series you did last month on 'victims of crime and tragedy'? Do you, by any chance, have the notes of the interview you did with the victims of that tragic crash that killed Doctor Tom Mitchum and others?"

"Of course I have. I was always advised to hold on to my notes, but why do you ask?"

"Well, I have been talking to his widow and she feels that something is not quite right with his death. Although it has been recorded as an accident, due in all probability, to mechanical failure. I am just wondering if you sensed anything unusual during your interview with Mrs Mitchum?"

"I think that of all the interviews that I did, her one was the most draining. Up to his death, according to her, they lived, what I would call, the most boring existence of all – a bit like the film, 'The Stepford Wives'. He did his work in the clinic as regular as clockwork. Living and working by the clock. She was the dutiful wife at home keeping the home in strict order, with no children to impinge on it. Then suddenly everything changes and she begins to question and challenge what has really been happening in their lives."

"Tell me more. What exactly did she say?"

"Hold on there and I will get my notes and I can tell you exactly." said Shirley.

Five minutes later Shirley had produced the notes of her interview with Beth Mitchum.

"Now as I said, on the face of it everything was fine, even when Beth had reason to question events, she always accepted Tom's version. For example, on at least three different occasions in the previous year, she believed she had seen Tom's car in different parts of the city when Tom was or should have been with clients. In actual fact she did question him on what she believed to be a certain sighting. On that occasion, he asked her to ring the matron to confirm that he was definitely at a meeting in the clinic with her and the assistant matron at the time that Beth said she had seen the car. There were many other incidences like that. On each such occasion, Tom denied any knowledge and Beth accepted his word. Now, following his death she has too much time to think about these things again and in her depressed grief she is thinking the worst."

"Would you be a 'Stepford Wife', just for once and do me a big favor, Babe?" Eddie cajoled, "Would you extract the issues that Beth brought up in the interview and jot them down on a sheet for me, like the ones you have just told me. I have asked her to do something similar. I want to be sure we missed nothing." he ducked the cushion that Shirley had fired at him.

"You know Eddie, at this stage, I am having serious doubts about our possible marriage. It might be harder for me to change you than I originally thought. However, giving you the benefit of the doubt – on this occasion only – I would love to!"

"You're an angel. I will do the same for you some day! Oh and by the way, we got the final replies from our request to all of the clinics in the state regarding Alice Newman-Becky Mason and all were negative. According to the replies neither Alice nor Becky are, or have ever been, residents in any of the facilities."

"So where is she?" Shirley wondered. "Unless she is

dead, and I have checked up on that. She can't just have disappeared into thin air, can she?"

"Maybe she is or was admitted under a false name. I remember that old professor up in the college mentioned something about relatives registering patients under false names in order to hide them away. Why don't you call him and, using your charm, see if you can get him to find the names of the ten patients that he said that Tom was trying to help and in particular, the one he succeeded in having transferred into his care. He seems to be the kind of guy who just might keep this kind of file."

"What a brilliant detective you are, my Darling. Now I know the world is safe as long as you, my warrior in shining armor, are on my case."

Chapter 40

"So what's on your mind?" asked the Chief, as Eddie sat opposite him in the Chief's office. "It had better be important as I am on my way to a meeting with the Commissioner in fifteen minutes' time."

"Well basically it concerns the accident on the freeway last October and in a way it also touches on the Gregg Newman case," Eddie replied

"But both of those cases are closed!" the Chief countered.

"I know, but you were a cop before becoming Chief and once a cop always a cop, so you will know what it means to 'have an itch' about something. Well I have an itch about this and I want permission to follow up on it."

"Eddie, I am going to meet the Commissioner to talk about our backlog of work and our shortage of men on the ground and the ongoing row about the shambolic state of the precinct. How we are to work efficiently in a place where we have to share desks and have only three interview rooms? How can I justify one of my top men wasting time on an itch?"

"Maybe it is more than an itch Chief," Eddie suggested. "Tom Mitchum's widow has raised a number of questions that, in my opinion, need to be followed up. That would initially entail questioning staff at the clinic and obtaining CCTV tapes, if they still have them. A maximum timeframe would be a day or two. At the moment, due to staff shortages in specialist areas, I am stuck in my workload awaiting a number of reports before I can proceed."

"OK, as long as I have known you Eddie you have seldom been wrong. You have a nose for getting to the truth. Just keep me posted and don't let your case load falter."

On returning to his office Eddie asked Maria to come into his office.

"Looks like you are going to get your own way, as usual," he said to her. "I have come around to your way of thinking regarding the accident that killed Doctor Mitchum."

"Well that's an about-turn, if ever I saw one," said Maria, "So what changed your mind? Since I couldn't?"

"I suppose I have been thinking of what his widow has been saying and I realize that she obviously knew her husband better that any of us or thought she did, and we jumped to an apparently obvious conclusion. Something is not right."

"That sure does make a lot of sense in my books. So

what is the deal?"

"I have had a meeting with the Chief and he has agreed for us to spend two days following up on our concerns, but we are not to drop our workload! So with such a short timeframe we need to be hyper-efficient."

"How about I take the widow and you take the clinic and this evening correlate our findings?" said Maria.

"Good thinking. Let's get at it."

As soon as Maria had left the office Eddie rang Sue Smyth, matron at the clinic.

"Good morning, matron," began Eddie. "My name is Detective Eddie McGrane. You may remember we met in connection with the tragic death of your chief psychiatrist, some time ago."

"Yes indeed, I well remember. You were very discreet in dealing with that awful tragedy, and what can I do for you, detective?"

"Well, Doctor Mitchum's widow has been in to see us and has raised a number of personal issues regarding her late husband and to allay her fears we need to talk to a few of your staff. Just to clarify things for her."

"Certainly, I see no problem with that. Just who exactly would you like to talk to, detective?"

"Initially we would like to talk to his PA or assistant,

whatever he or she is called. Then possibly the receptionist and finally the person in charge of maintenance/administration. A right mixed bag, you might say," Eddie laughed.

"My goodness, it certainly is, but as I said, we have no problem as long as it is done very discreetly. We wouldn't want to unnerve any of our patients, now would we?" replied matron. "When would you like to start?"

"How about today?" replied Eddie. "We have a very short timeframe in which to help the widow in this regard so your help is very much appreciated. Can you make these people available and in the interest of, as you say discretion, perhaps you could allocate a quiet place for us to conduct the interviews?"

"Well, it is really very short notice but the sooner it is over the better. I have had a number of chats with Beth, Tom's widow, and I appreciate how she is feeling. They were such a united couple. At times, I believe we are better off if each partner has an identity of their own. It is so devastating for the survivor in such deaths as Tom's. Let me see who is available and I will get back to you within the hour."

Chapter 41

As soon as he replaced the phone Eddie lifted it again and called Bill Johnson in Traffic. "Hi Bill, Eddie McGrane here, once again."

"Well well, if it isn't my old pal Detective Eddie McGrane. What can I do for you today Eddie? I presume you are looking for something? Why else would you lower yourself to fraternize with us lowly denizens of the Traffic Corps?"

"I always felt that you should have been in PR. You have a unique talent for making a person feel wanted!" Eddie jibed.

"Yes, I too believe that my talents are wasted here. Now how can I help you?"

"You remember the crash on the freeway that killed the psychiatrist, last October? Well the widow is asking questions and the Chief has asked me to take another look, not at the accident itself – that has been wrapped up by your good self. No, it's the behaviour of the psychiatrist himself. Apparently for a guy that lived by routine he seems, at least in the widow's opinion, to have had a few questions to answer."

"So how can we help?" said a puzzled Bill.

"I was hoping that you still had the CCTV tapes of the day of the accident and better still if you had any tapes of the previous few days. I would just like to have another look. The day we were with you our focus was different. We just wanted to prove that the psychiatrist was the person who got into the car. Now we are looking for anything that may have been out of the ordinary as far as his behaviour was concerned."

"Hold on a minute and I will check."

Five minutes later he was back on the phone. "You were always lucky, Eddie. Yes, we have the tapes for the day before the accident and the day of the accident. Unfortunately, I can't let you have them but feel free to come over and view them here, at any time."

"Great news, I'll be over in ten minutes. I owe you one for this. That makes it two that I owe you now." Eddie chirped.

Fifteen minutes later he was ensconced in front of a large screen viewing the CCTV footage of the entrance to the clinic's reception area. Nothing seemed to be out of place. People came and went as they would in any hospital or clinic. The second tape was of the car park and again everything appeared to be normal, not too many comings and goings here. The third tape was of the delivery area and apparently the staff car parking area also. This was a more active area with vans and trucks making food deliveries for the kitchens and also laundry collections and deliveries. Eddie counted twenty numbered parking spots. However, the first thing that struck Eddie was the difficulty in seeing all of the parked cars as, in many instances the view was obscured by one if not two trucks. This applied to the parking spots number one and two, the spots nearest to the avenue. The doors to the delivery and laundry section were between spots two and three. As a result, vans and trucks were often parked between the cars parked in spot one and two and the admin building where the CCTV camera was fitted. By the time he finished viewing the first day's tapes his eyes were sore and his spirits low as he hadn't found anything that he felt warranted investigation.

As he started to view the tapes of the day of the accident, he decided to skip the tape of the public car park and went straight to the tape of the entrance area as this was the area that interested him most on his first viewing. Again there appeared to be nothing unusual.

He then selected the tape of the delivery area. Again there was nothing unusual until he came to the footage showing Doctor Mitchum running to his car and speeding off down the avenue. So what was he missing? he asked himself. Time was running out on him but he needed to be sure, he needed to visit the clinic and see for himself.

Chapter 42

When he got back to his office there were a number of messages awaiting him. The one he was waiting for was from the matron. Yes, she had a schedule of interviews lined up for him with the staff in question. The first one scheduled for two fifteen, it was now one forty. That ended his hopes of a lunch. It would take all his time to make it to the clinic in less than thirty-five minutes.

As he walked in to the clinic reception, matron was waiting for him.

"Good afternoon detective. I have allocated a quiet office here where you should have complete privacy. Come with me and I will show you. I have suggested that you talk to Amy Stone our head receptionist first and then Stella Maher, Doctor Mitchum's PA secondly. You see Amy will be on her break at that time and Stella will then be free. Finally, Jim Salmon, our maintenance supervisor will be free. I hope this arrangement will meet with your approval?" said matron.

"Absolutely perfect. As far as these people are concerned, we are just reviewing the accident so that we can install improved safety precautions for the future." Eddie replied.

"Yes, I appreciate your discretion detective. I will send Amy down to you immediately."

"Hi Amy," said Eddie as a slim built young girl entered the room. "My name is Eddie, Eddie McGrane. I am a detective with your local precinct. We are trying to examine the circumstances surrounding Doctor Mitchum's tragic death. I know it was some time ago but you never know what we might have missed when the tragedy happened. We do miss things from time to time so I am hoping that you might trigger a memory or something that points us in a different direction. Let's start with Doctor Mitchum's daily routine."

"Well, normally you could set your watch by Doctor Mitchum's routine." Amy began. "He would be at his desk each morning before anyone else, usually that meant an eight o'clock start and he always finished at six o'clock. Apart from taking a one-hour lunch break which he took in the staff restaurant between one o'clock and two o' clock, he never left his office."

"I understand that he carried out a private practice from his office also." observed Eddie. "So how did he manage that?"

"Yes, on Tuesdays, Wednesdays and Fridays, he held his private clinics. On Tuesdays and Fridays from four o'clock until six o'clock and on Wednesdays until eight o'clock. He was very strict on these timings. When the client arrived I would call his office and send them down, precisely on the hour. He would see only three clients each evening which meant that he had ten minutes to write up each file."

"That all seems to be very well organized," Eddie noted. "Do you recall anything peculiar on the day of the accident or was it routine, as you mentioned?"

"No, I can't recall seeing him leave that evening, which was unusual. You see he would always, or almost always, wish whoever was on reception, a very enjoyable weekend. I must have just hopped out for a minute and missed him."

"Thank you very much for your time and your help." said Eddie. "That is exactly the kind of information we were missing. I think that I now know Doctor Mitchum better already. If you think of anything else, please call me."

No sooner had Amy left the office when Stella Maher knocked on the door. Having introduced himself and given the story about checking up on the proposed changes to the protective barriers on the avenue, Eddie began.

"So Stella, tell me how long had you been working as

Doctor Mitchum's PA?"

"Well I don't think you could call me his PA, although I did act in some way as his assistant but not always. He did look after at least fifty per cent of what he did. I just looked after his mail, his schedule and basic administration. I joined the clinic three years ago but it was only in the last six months that I was working with Doctor Mitchum."

"Did you notice any change in his behaviour during that time?"

"Most people viewed Doctor Mitchum as a paragon of peace and tranquility, but I found him to be tense and at times irritable over what I would consider small matters."

"Can you expand on that please?" Eddie probed, "What kind of issues come to your mind?"

"For example, sometimes the clinic would get their schedule of patients mixed up, or the patients would be late in arriving which upset his private client schedule. In such cases he would be very tense and let whoever was responsible know all about it. This was a side to him that most people never saw."

"That seems to contradict most people's opinion of him." said Eddie. "You have been most helpful and thank you for coming in to talk to us." As he ushered her out of the room.

No sooner had Stella left than a small bustling

bald-headed little man arrived at the office.

"Jim Salmon, I presume?" said Eddie. "Please take a seat. I'm sure matron filled you in on our concern about the security barriers on the avenue."

"And about time sir, if I may say so." responded Jim. "Those barriers went out with the flood. They wouldn't stop a snow ball. I have been saying that ever since I arrived here twelve months ago. Do you think they would listen to me? No, the cost would be too much they said. I wonder how much value they would now put on poor Doctor Mitchum's life. He would be alive now if they had listened to me."

"Tell me Jim," Eddie interrupted. "How would you rate Doctor Mitchum as a driver? I assume you saw him come and go often enough to form an opinion."

"Well, normally I would consider him a menace on the road. If the limit was fifty miles per hour, he would do no more than forty miles per hour. He was the original slow-coach. You know, the kind of drivers that force other drivers to take chances just to pass him out. However, once or twice he amazed me by leaving rubber on the car park as he sped away. Particularly if he was late or if his car had been blocked in by a delivery van or lorry."

"But surely he had his own parking spot? Number twelve I believe. So such an occurrence would be highly unlikely, would it not?" pursued Eddie.

"Of course, that would be the case if he stuck to his allocated space. However shortly after I arrived he asked me to allocate space number one instead. I pointed out that that particular space was adjacent to where the delivery trucks and vans would park. However, he was adamant and asked me to make the change for him."

"Did he give you any reason for the change?"

"Well, the first time it came to my attention was the Friday. It always seemed to be on a Friday. When I saw a woman drive his car out of the clinic. I immediately called him and he told me that his wife would want to borrow his car from time to time and that she liked it to be parked facing the hill. I assumed she wasn't a very proficient driver."

"This is very important Jim. Can you recall when exactly this happened?"

"I'm afraid not. As you can see, that parking spot is far from my office, but it did happen on at least six or seven occasions that I can remember."

As soon as Jim had left, Eddie texted Maria.

Chapter 43

When Maria called to Beth she couldn't believe the change that had taken place in her. She looked as if she had aged at least ten years and appeared worn and disheveled. Her hair looked as if it hadn't seen a comb in days, if not weeks. The sitting room that had been so warm, too warm, and welcoming was today cold and lifeless with stacks of papers and files scattered everywhere.

"So good of you to come." said Beth. "Sorry for the state of the house but I seem to have no time to sort anything out and I have nobody to help me." She apologized as she began to move papers and files from the chairs and floor. "Here, sit here please while I put the kettle on and we can have a cup of coffee and then have a good long chat. You have no idea how confused I seem to have become, almost overnight."

"Don't worry Beth, this is quite normal." Maria explained, "You have had a terrible shock and it is very common in those kinds of circumstances for a person to become disorientated and suffer temporary memory loss. You just relax, make the coffee, and when you are ready, you can tell me all that is worrying you."

Ten minutes later as they were sitting in front of the empty fireplace, having coffee and cookies, Maria said, "Tell me a bit about yourself Beth. For instance, tell me where do you come from? And how did Tom and you meet up?"

"Well, I grew up in a farm in Windward with my brother. He went off to join the army and sadly didn't survive his second tour of duty in Afghanistan. It broke my father's heart and he passed away three years ago, my Mom predeceased him four years earlier. In the meantime, I had enrolled in Charlestown College where I studied History and Physics. It was then that I met Tom. Tom, beautiful sincere Tom. Oh how I fell for him – hook, line and sinker – maybe not everybody's cup of tea but oh how I loved him."

"You must miss him terribly," murmured Maria.

"Oh yes, I do but now I am beginning to wonder did I really know him at all. Looking back now I think I must have been sleepwalking not to notice changes in Tom's behaviour. There are so many other things that I can't explain to myself."

"Let's take things one at a time," Maria suggested, "and see if we can make sense of any or all of them. For instance, tell me when did you first notice a change in Tom?"

"I have known Tom for over ten years and was married to him for six of those years. I honestly thought that I knew his every breath and thought. Now I don't know what is real and what is in my imagination."

"But in what way exactly did Tom change?"

"As I mentioned, at first I was not aware of a specific change in Tom and thought that I was the one who was acting strangely, possibly spending too much time on my own. However, since the accident I have been looking more closely at our lives in the past year and I began to realize that it was Tom, and not I, that had changed."

"That must have been very upsetting and worrying for you."

"My doctor says that it is just part of the grieving process. The initial shock, followed by the anger, followed by the doubts but when you see the personal items that the clinic delivered to me, and I have only looked at a few of them, you too will believe me that something is not right. I already mentioned the purchase of that gun thing. Then I find boxes of tablets and Tom very seldom took tablets."

"Would it be possible that they were a supply for the clinic?"

"But why would they need such a supply and why would they be in with his personal items? I remember once sending his suit to the cleaners and checking in the pockets

I found one unopened condom. Of course at that time I fully believed Tom's explanation that he had found it on the floor when a client had left and that he had intended binning it." Beth sighed. "Now I am not so sure."

"Can you take me back to the changes you saw in Tom? Were they physical or attitude changes? And did you ever challenge him on them?"

"That is precisely what I mean, before I could ask Tom anything and we could have a great discussion about it. But then in the last twelve months or so he would snap at me and tell me I was getting paranoid about little things. So I suppose it was a change in attitude that I first noticed. Then I noticed that he was getting a lot of headaches." said Beth.

"Did he say why he felt he was getting headaches or anything like that?"

"Always it was put down to pressure of work but he always had the same work load. And he used to say that he could do the work of the clinic in his sleep! So where was the pressure?"

"Looking back now Beth, do you have any idea what exactly started this change in him and when it all started?"

"I have racked my brain to try and remember and the only thing that I think might have something to do with it occurred last January. Tom had been helping out in a clinic upstate a few years ago and got very agitated about a case he had brought to the attention of the State Governor. I think it was something about people who were in clinics who should not have been there. I might have this a bit mixed up, but it was something like that. Anyway, as nothing was happening to his appeal, he drove up to the Governor's office last January, but when he came back he told me that his intervention had been well worthwhile. He later mentioned that as a result of his stand, he had succeeded in getting one of the people transferred into his care, up at the clinic."

"You wouldn't remember if he mentioned that person's name, would you?"

"Oh no, Tom was the height of discretion in matters like that. Anyway it was around that time that Tom became a bit distant with me and kind of touchy if I mentioned his tiredness or his losing weight; things that normally we would have no problem discussing. He nearly had a seizure one day when I suggested he visit his own doctor. Mind you he eventually did visit him but of course never told me that he was diagnosed with high blood pressure."

Just then, Maria's phone buzzed – it was a text from Eddie. "Ask Beth did she often visit Tom at the clinic and did she ever have occasion to go up there and borrow his car. I will see you in my office in an hour."

Chapter 44

"Tell me a bit about the clinic, Beth. How you got on with the staff up there?" Maria continued.

"The clinic? My God that was Tom's sanctuary. I think I visited it only once in all our time here. That was his workplace and I knew I would not be welcome if I did want to visit. In Tom's view a wife's place was in the home. It certainly was not in visiting her husband's place of work."

"So how did you share the one car you had?" asked Maria. "I assume that Tom took it to work each day, so how did you manage? I suppose you would call to the clinic and take it while Tom was working and return it in time for him to come home."

"No, I would never take the car while Tom was working. I would always use public transport. That was the way Tom liked it and to be honest, I had no problem with that."

"Talking about the car, you did mention that you thought you had seen it in the city on a few occasions when Tom was working. Can you recall exactly where and when these incidents happened?"

"Not really. I think I had mentioned that they were probably on Fridays, the day I attended my course in the library which, as I mentioned, is up near the university. So it could only have been on a Friday that I would have been up there and that was the locality I thought I had seen the car in. As you know, Tom said that it was impossible and that it was probably the car of one of the university professors that he knew and who owned a similar type and color car."

"OK, now let's get on to the Taser gun. Did you manage to find any paperwork in relation to the purchase and payment?"

"Yes, I have found the credit card details and our bank is to get back to me with details of the date and vendor. However, there is no trace of the gun in his personal items and no paperwork. I will have to wait until the bank rings me. They said it could be fourteen days. I have also asked them for details regarding some other purchases from an electronic shop and a ladies' shop. Again I am awaiting their call back."

"What about all the items that the clinic returned? Have you had time to examine them yet?"

"To be honest with you, at this stage, I dread looking at them for fear of what I might find. I have put his client files away safely until I find out how to deal with them. I am not too sure if I should return them to the clients or to the clinic. I certainly don't want to be reading other people's problems. I have enough of my own. Regarding all the other bits and pieces, I hope to get to sorting them this week, if I can find it in my heart to look at them."

"OK Beth, I think we have covered a lot of ground today." Maria concluded, "Is it ok if I call again tomorrow to follow up on what we have teased out? If tomorrow doesn't suit it will probably be at least a fortnight before I can get back again to see you."

"Certainly, tomorrow would be perfect and I really appreciate you taking the time to visit me. It means an awful lot to me just to know that someone is listening to my worries."

When Maria got back to the station she went straight to Eddie's office.

"Well, how did you get on?" asked Eddie. "I hope my text didn't interrupt your questioning."

"Not at all, I had a very fruitful visit and feel that I know Beth better by now. She seems to be waking up to the fact that her beloved husband was a controller of the first degree. She couldn't sneeze without his permission. So what is behind your question?"

"As you know, everyone said that Tom was a very detailed man. Everything had to be in its place and that applied to his parking spot into which he reversed each day.

Each senior staff member had a designated parking place in the clinic. The most senior staff had the places nearest the entrance to the clinic and as such, Tom had pride of place straight outside the door. However sometime within the last twelve months he requested to the maintenance supervisor that he be given the place furthest away from the entrance – the most unwanted parking spot in the entire parking lot. His excuse was that his wife wanted to borrow the car from time to time, and it suited her to have the spot nearest to the avenue."

"But why would he do that? That doesn't make any sense. I asked Beth the questions that you suggested. Her response was that it would have been more likely for her to go to the moon than go to the clinic to see Tom or indeed to borrow his car. Something is very rotten here," Maria suggested.

"To add to that, I recall looking at the CCTV tape of the day of the accident and if you recall, it showed Tom running out of the clinic, jumping into his car and REVERSING out of the parking spot but he always reversed into his space – isn't that what we were told? Could it be that someone else parked the car?" Eddie wondered.

"That could well be the answer. According to Beth, Tom's change towards her started about a year ago when he got involved in challenging the state on the retention of patients in psychiatric facilities beyond the court retention periods for these patients. According to Beth he had become obsessed with the patient who had been transferred to his care and was out to use that to prove his contention that all such patients should be reassessed at least every three years. In the case in question his view was that the patient should never have been committed at all."

Chapter 45

Later that evening, as Eddie and Shirley were painting Eddie's apartment. Eddie having finally succumbed to her suggestion that they both get involved in redecoration. Shirley challenged him, "You seem to be very preoccupied this evening, Eddie. What's bothering you? I hope it is not the color I picked for the bedroom. If it is, we can always change it to black, it might be an appropriate alternative, and would suit your frame of mind!"

"No Babe, it's nothing to do with the apartment. I just love the colors you have chosen. It's that damn case of the doctor from the clinic who died. Nothing seems to make sense and the Chief has given only partial support to my concerns. I can't seem to get it out of my head."

"I thought that that case was done and dusted and, by the way, our doddering old professor from Charleston texted me this morning to say that he had checked back on his notes and the name of the patient that Tom had 'rescued', was Sarah Silver. So that closed that door for me. I had hoped it would have been Alice, but I still don't believe in coincidences and never will."

"Look Shirley, my mind isn't in the painting tonight. Why not call it a day or night, clean ourselves up and go for a walk by the lake? The way I feel right now I am liable to paint the floor instead of the ceiling!" Eddie sighed.

"Great idea, I thought you would never think of it. My mind isn't fully in it either and besides, we have actually finished two rooms already. Granted it has taken us all of three weeks to do it, but we are in no hurry, are we? You are not going to spring a surprise on me any day soon and propose?" Shirley teased.

"You know Shirley, I said it before and I will say it again – you are a tonic. Just when I think I have a problem, you snap me out of it by reminding me of what it would be like to have you as my wife – the thought is unthinkable! Come on and make yourself semi-respectable and think about serious matters, like food."

When they tried to get into their usual restaurants they found that it being Saturday night, every place was full, and even with his usual influence, none of them could get a table for them. Eventually they settled for a burger and fries takeaway which they had while sitting on a lakeside bench.

"Shirley, being the investigative journalist that you are, tell me what you really think of the case of Doctor Tom Mitchum?" Eddie began.

"Tell me the up to date details and I will give you

my opinion," Shirley said as she blew on a French fry and popped it in her mouth.

"OK. Here we have a renowned psychiatrist who is, apparently, happily married for a number of years. He is a stickler for detail in every aspect of his life, according to all and sundry. And then, in the last twelve months or so, seems to have become a different person. While appearing to be the same person on the outside."

"In what way?"

Eddie then went on to detail what the widow had said and to give examples of the change in Doctor Mitchum's behaviour regarding the parking space and the apparent sighting of his car in strange places by his wife, and in particular the issue of the odd purchases made by him.

"To me it has all the hallmarks of a man in midlife crisis, who is having an affair," Shirley decided. "However, I know that from what you tell me of the doctor and his wife, that that would be a mind-blowing conclusion. He just doesn't fit the profile. But that's what it looks like. Maybe, just maybe, he was involved with one of his patients. It has been known that sometimes patients and their doctors cross the line of propriety and stray into a personal relationship. That might explain the purchases from the ladies' boutique. It would not however explain the Taser gun, unless he purchased that for the person in question for his or her protection. But that sounds off the wall. A doctor would never do that I am sure. Other than that I have no idea."

"Now I know why you are so successful at your job – you think outside of the box. Yes, the involvement of a third party might explain a lot. I need to visit the clinic again and have a further chat with matron," Eddie reflected.

On his way into the station the following morning, Eddie took a detour and called in to the clinic. As he was getting out of his car, matron had just left her car and was walking across to reception.

"Good morning detective, and what brings you to our clinic this morning?" said matron. "I had hoped that we would have given you all the help we could up to now."

"You and your staff have been more than helpful. However, I still feel that something is not right. Do you have fifteen minutes to hear my problem?" Eddie replied.

"Come on in to my office and we can have a coffee and you can tell me what it is that concerns you." said matron.

"Well, in the first place it appears from, all we have been told, that Doctor Mitchum was a very stable and predictable man and had been ever since he started working here. In actual fact, people have said that he was predictable to the point of boredom – that was until sometime in the past twelve months when he appeared to change, in many little ways."

"Could that be related to the additional workload that Tom, I mean Doctor Mitchum, had taken on? You do know that he was much in demand all over the state for consultations and giving lectures. That pressure of work would surely cause anyone to deviate from their normal routine, don't you think?" Matron suggested.

"Possibly, but he was always doing that kind of work. No, I feel that something happened in his life within the last twelve months that had an effect on him," Eddie countered.

"I could look up the list of patients he attended over the past year and see if anything strikes me as unusual. Of course, you appreciate that I could not divulge any patient's names or treatment details."

"I fully appreciate that matron. But having said that, I understand that around that time Doctor Mitchum had a patient transferred from some other clinic upstate into his care. Sarah Silver was her name. Can you tell me if she is still a patient here?"

"Sorry detective, but under no circumstances could I even discuss that without a court order. Can you tell me where you got that information?"

"It was actually his professor up in Charlestown who

mentioned it in conversation. Anyway apparently that was over a year ago and Tom's behaviour change seems to have been only in the past twelve months. I fully appreciate that you can't comment on that, matron, but I am grasping at straws, as it were. Anyway, thank you very much for taking the time to see me." Eddie replied, as he left the office.

When he got into the station, Maria was waiting for him.

"Late date again, Eddie. You are getting too old for that carry on. Why don't you marry the girl and stop messing around? In the meantime, Beth wants us out to see her again, says it's important."

"OK let's go before the Chief finds out that we are gone," Eddie whispered.

Chapter 46

"You know Eddie, six months ago I didn't even know that this part of the city existed. Now I could drive around it blindfolded," said Maria, as they approached Beth's house.

"Thank you so much again for coming all the way out here to see me again." Beth greeted them. "I do feel that I have found something unusual in Tom's belongings. As I mentioned at your last visit, I was checking our financial position with our bank manager. Well since then I have been going through some of his papers. But I haven't gone near his filing cabinet as yet. God alone knows what I am liable to find there. Anyway, as I was looking through his personal diary I came across an entry 'SS this evening five p.m. to six p.m.' this appeared on a number of Fridays. Sometimes the times were different, like 'SS twelve thirty p.m. to three thirty p.m.' on the day he died it said 'four p.m. to six p.m.'. These entries stretched back at least seven or eight months. So what does it mean?"

"Could it be that it was just to remind him of some sort of appointments? He did have appointments with his doctor, as you found out after he had the accident," Eddie suggested.

"But why would he have that in his personal diary? Surely something like that would be in his work diary?" Beth argued. "It doesn't make sense to me. Could it be something to do with the yoga classes? What do you think?"

"I don't know," said Eddie, "but, for a start, let's check the times of the yoga classes with the clinic," as he called the clinic on his cell phone.

"Hi matron, sorry to bother you again but we are here with Tom's widow and we are trying to clear up a few issues for her. Can you tell me what days and times the yoga classes are held in the clinic. You know the ones you were telling me that Tom had arranged for one of his patients to organize and run?" Eddie queried.

When he was finished talking to matron he told Beth that the classes were held every Wednesday and Friday but always from five p.m. to six p.m. They would never be held at any other time.

"Do you remember that I asked you to document the details of all of the issues you noted in the bank statement and the occasions on which you thought you had seen his car in unusual places, Beth? If you have the list we can check the days and the times against these entries in the diary," said Eddie.

"That's amazing. Look, every item on Beth's list coincides with an entry in the diary!" Maria pointed out.

"But what does it mean?" asked Beth.

"I honestly don't know what to make of it," said Eddie, "but I intend to find out. Beth, you mentioned that you haven't looked at Tom's filing cabinet yet. You previously mentioned that matron had indicated that the files of his private clients were in that cabinet and that the clinic had retained the files of the other patients. Those files that you now have are your property. Will you give us permission to examine them just to see if we can uncover whatever Tom was involved in? Hopefully it will be nothing."

"Certainly, by all means take the files. There are only about fifty in total, from what I am told." said Beth.

Over the next two hours Eddie and Maria scoured the files looking for anything that might cast light on Tom's change of behaviour. In the end they both agreed that looking at patient's files was one of the most depressing things they had ever done, and found nothing.

"Well that was a brilliant idea, was it not? Two wasted hours and nothing to show," Maria sighed. "Now what are you looking so perplexed for?"

"I am trying to find what we are missing and I think I have found it. Go back and take out the file for Sarah

Silver, the patient he had transferred to his care."

"Not much in it." said Maria, "It refers only to the detox program."

"Precisely! That's my point." said Eddie. "Look, the first entry is when she arrived at the clinic and from then on the entries refer only to the program. A program that lasted for approximately twelve months. No further entries. I wonder why? Is it alright if we take these files with us, Beth? We will bring them back to you tomorrow."

"That's no problem." said Beth.

"I wonder if the clinic had a file on her? After all she was technically transferred to the clinic albeit under the care of Tom." Maria said.

"Even if they had, it would take a court order to get a look at it and we sure as hell haven't sufficient reason to suggest that." Eddie replied.

"Ok Beth, we are going to have to have to leave you now. Can I ask you to check and double-check to see if Tom would have kept other notes or files or records, anywhere else in the house? You have my cell number. Ring me if you find anything. In the meantime, we will see what we can find out from Sarah Silver's file."

On their way back to the station they decided that they would spend just one more night trying to help Beth.

After that it would be back to their normal days' work – keeping the Chief off their backs.

"Have you finished the painting of your apartment yet?" asked Maria, "If not we better go to my place, ok?"

"Good, my place is still a work in progress. Should be finished next week. Then will come the task of fitting it out. Shirley has big plans." Eddie laughed.

"I bet she has!" said Maria.

Chapter 47

As they sat around the kitchen table in Maria's place, Eddie began. "I had a chance to read the first part of Sarah Silver's file and it appears that when Sarah came to the clinic she was highly dependent on sedatives. According to the first day's entry, she had been prescribed a very addictive and powerful sedative from the first day of her committal to the Haven Clinic and Tom's final entry on that first day was that, in his opinion, she would need an aggressive detox program coupled with a whole new diet regime. Her weight was recorded as eighty-four pounds. His notes said that he would be putting a dedicated team together to work with her and envisaged it would take up to one full year to get her back to physical normality. Then he would work on her mental state; a very daunting task, he predicted."

"So how did the program progress?" Maria asked.

"I only got as far as month three and as far as I could discern, it was tedious – two steps forward and one step back but overall progress seemed to exceed his initial expectations. In fairness to the doctor, he seemed to be patience personified, calm and sure. He seems to have taken to her in a big way. Here, you take the file and read on from where I have marked. While you are doing that, I will try and piece together what we have so far and see if we are getting any kind of picture."

An hour later Maria called Eddie, "Have a look at this entry. It's at about month five:

'Sarah is making good progress and beginning to wonder who is paying for her stay at the clinic – I must find out!'

I wonder did he ever find out. Now that's an interesting angle. Where was the money coming from?"

"That's another question for matron to answer. If she will." Eddie replied. "Take a break from the reading. I will take over. God, but it's so boring reading about doses and reaction and apparent progress only to see it fall back time and time again."

"What you need is a nice cup of coffee. I might even find something nice to go with it."

As they sat enjoying some of Maria's apple pie, Eddie remarked. "I never knew you could cook pie like this. If the Chief finds out what we are doing at least you will have another job to go to. This is the best apple pie I have had – today!" Eddie laughed.

"Anything new?" Maria asked, as thirty minutes later Eddie closed the file.

"Well firstly, at the end of year one it appears that Sarah was almost drug free but, as he commented, she was becoming more and more dependent on the team. She had put on twenty-eight pounds in weight and was having sensible conversations with Tom. According to the final note, she was ready for psychological assessment. The only problem is that while the file is very comprehensive on medical jargon and the withdrawal progress, it is very light on who or what Sarah was. There has to be another file somewhere." Eddie mused.

"Well, if matron cleared out his office and returned all to Beth then it has to be in the house somewhere – but where? Perhaps it was with him in the car and is now gone forever."

"Hold it! That's it! Where is his briefcase? He didn't have anything in his hand when, on the CCTV tape, we saw him running to the car, so it must be either at the clinic or in the house. Beth has been concentrating only on what the clinic returned – not what was or is already in the house. I'll ring her in the morning. It's too late now to disturb her. Remember, she mentioned that she takes a sleeping tablet around nine o'clock every evening in an effort to get some sleep."

"I thought you said that we were only going to give this one more night and then tell Beth that we could do no more for her?" Maria argued.

"Well it just means a phone call to matron and another to Beth."

"Really!" said Maria, "You can't let go, Eddie, can you?"

Next morning Eddie called Beth and asked her to check if Tom had left his briefcase at the clinic or was it in the house. And when she had looked, to let him know. He also called matron and asked her if she could let him know what the procedure was in regard for the payment of fees for committed patients. Was it the state who paid? Matron replied that it would always be the family or person who had applied to the court who would be responsible for all such fees. Normally these fees would be arranged with a bank to pay them directly to the clinic either monthly or quarterly.

Two hours later Mary rang back to say that she had found Tom's briefcase, under the bed but that it was locked.

"Great, Beth." said Eddie. "Hold on to it and we will call out to you this evening around seven o'clock, if that is alright with you?"

Chapter 48

That evening, with Beth's permission, it didn't take Eddie very long to open the briefcase. Inside they found, amongst other bits and pieces, a number of files and a daily journal. One of the files, a very thick file, had the name 'Sarah Silver' on it.

"Let's start with the file, he suggested, and see what kind of entries are in it."

"It is completely different from the other file. This one seems to be a record of sessions with the psychiatrist, nothing to do with medicine. It appears to commence where the other file ends." Maria noted.

"I'll start with the file and you start with the journal," said Eddie, "and see where it leads us. I must admit that I feel like a voyeur, reading other people's problems. It must be very difficult for psychiatrists to remain even half sane, spending day after day listening to real and perceived problems."

Two hours later they took a break to compare notes. Eddie's evaluation of what he had read so far was that the file was no more than a very clinical record of every session the doctor had with Sarah over the past twelve months or so. The first month appeared to be no more than a record of unanswered questions as the doctor tried to get her to confide in him and reveal something about herself. However, during the second month there seemed to be more of a connection between patient and doctor with the doctor revealing some of his own identity in an effort to encourage her to do likewise. It was slow work as Sarah seemed to have problems remembering her own background. This the doctor attributed to the effect of the sedation she was under for so long. At one stage he noted that his research had indicated the real possibility that, as a result of the prolonged sedation, it was possible that she would never remember her full history.

By month three he had succeeded in getting her to walk with him in the clinic garden which, according to the file, was a huge step forward. He followed up on this by getting her to start writing down any and all of her thoughts no matter how disconnected they might be. According to the notes he made, these were very revealing. He didn't however say in what way they were revealing. From that point onward however the notes talked of great progress in their relationship, with Sarah expressing confidence and regard for the doctor. However there seemed to be no notes on how this improved situation was expressed in terms of Sarah's mental stability.

Shortly afterwards, Sarah was well enough to start taking yoga classes which were held once a week for patients of the clinic. She also started using the gym and spent many an hour each day in building up her strength. In no time her weight started to return to normal.

By month four, Sarah had apparently suggested that, as she had done a course in yoga previously, she would stand in for the teacher on an occasion when the teacher was unable to attend. The doctor noted that this had had a very positive effect on Sarah. It restored her confidence, while providing a service for the clinic. The doctor noted that he was now confident that his treatment was working, and reiterated his opinion that she should never have been committed to any clinic. She is very angry, but normal, he noted. He also noted that 'Sarah was very animated and excited' at her achievement – she even gave him a hug! Up to then she had avoided all physical contact with the doctor. Having discussed the progress with the full clinic team, he suggested that Sarah be given the task of developing the yoga classes on a commercial basis by opening it up, not only to patients, but to the local community from where there might be interest. Apparently this was approved. According to the notes, this had a very positive effect on Sarah and, as she gained in self-confidence, she became more communicative and tactile. At times, like a child, she expressed the need to be hugged or touched by others, including the doctor. This was not acceptable to the doctor but he noted that he had to be careful not to undo all the good work that he had done by being seen to reject her.

"This is very interesting," said Eddie to Maria, interrupting her study of the journal. "All along we have been wondering who Sarah Silver was and our attempts to get matron to talk about her were met with the usual 'can't talk about a patient.' Now here we have her conducting public yoga classes. I think I have a job for Shirley when she gets home tonight. She always talked about taking up yoga."

Eddie yawned, "I think I've had enough for today. Let's leave it until tomorrow evening, if you are free, that is?"

"Yes, like you Eddie, I can't take too much of reading other people's thoughts and actions," Maria agreed. "Every word the patient used seems to have been analyzed. I don't know how psychiatrists ever remain sane or indeed how their spouses survive hyper-analysis! Every statement or comment must be thoroughly analyzed. Wow. I'd hate to have to live with that."

"One thing is becoming very clear," Eddie commented, "that as Sarah, the patient, improved Doctor Mitchum seems to have been drawn closer and closer to Sarah the person."

As soon as he got home Eddie called Shirley on her cell phone and filled her in on what he had unearthed about the mysterious Sarah Silver. He suggested that after her week away in the country researching the changes in social attitudes amongst the under thirties, she would appreciate an introduction to yoga sessions. Immediately she agreed to call the clinic and book in for a session the following evening.

Chapter 49

First thing the following morning Eddie reported to the Chief. "Well, I hope you haven't been wasting our time with the doctor's widow." growled the Chief, "Did you find what was itching you?"

"Not exactly," said Eddie, "but I did locate the area of the itch which is none other than our esteemed doctor. He doesn't appear to be exactly what he appears to be, if you get my drift. We have managed to get a look at some of his files; files relating to his private patients and in particular to the file relating to Sarah Silver."

"What do you mean exactly?"

"It appears that over the past few months his behaviour changed from that of a rigid way of life to one of unpredictability. This is mentioned by his widow and confirmed by his assistant. It also seems to coincide with the arrival of Sarah Silver, whose committal he had questioned, right up to the State Governor's office. He eventually got her released, from the Haven Clinic in Broadway, to his personal care in the Minerva Clinic."

"So what are you hinting at, Eddie? Do you think he committed suicide? Is that your guess?"

"To be honest Chief, I'm not sure what I am

postulating. Reading the file, it would seem that the patient-doctor relationship was drifting across the line at times. So the itch is still there and getting worse. Give me another day or so, we still have a lot of reading to do in his files."

The following morning Eddie and Shirley met up for an early breakfast at Nino's. Shirley hadn't arrived back at her apartment until well after midnight and Eddie had been putting in extra late hours at the painting just to surprise her.

"Before you ask Eddie, let me tell you you don't really want to know what our survey found out, do you?" said Shirley.

"Of course I do, Babe, but you are under thirty and I am under forty and we know that with the phenomena of social media, our attitudes are bound to have changed. That makes simple sense, doesn't it?" Eddie replied, trying to raise her.

"See? There you go again – jumping to conclusions as usual. Why are all men like that?" Shirley jibed, "For your information, detective, our attitudes, that is our deep-seated attitudes, are formed, by and large, in our family of origin. Someday, when you grow up, I will explain it all to you – in very simple terms." said Shirley.

"I know when I have met my equal," Eddie sighed

"Now, on a serious note, have you had any luck with the yoga class?"

"Yes, I spoke to a very efficient and pleasant Sarah Silver who has agreed to give me a free introductory session at five p.m. But, tell me, what am I looking for, precisely?"

"I'm not sure what you should be looking for, but I'm sure, a smart girl like you will think of something. Now unfortunately I have a boss to answer to and if I don't start solving some of the shit on my desk soon, I will be joining you on your junkets around the state. Remember, I have the tickets for tonight's ball game. Call for you at six thirty? You should be back from the yoga by then. And don't forget to shower!" Eddie called as he ducked the bread roll she had thrown at him.

Now that the Chief had given him a little more slack, he called Beth to see if it was ok for them to call again to continue their reading of the files. He then called Maria and filled her in on the chat he had had with the Chief and had penciled in two hours in which to finish with the file and journal.

When they arrived at Beth's she had the coffee ready for them and the files out on the table. Eddie was pleased to see that she looked much better, having obviously taken some time on her appearance.

"Good morning, officers," Beth greeted them. "You will be pleased to hear that I have an appointment to see a bereavement counsellor later on today – thanks to your suggestion. Just making the appointment makes me feel better. She sounded so kind and helpful. I just feel she will understand what I am going through."

"Delighted to hear that, Beth," said Maria. "You have gone through a very difficult time and nothing could prepare you for what has happened. Let us know how you get on."

Fifteen minutes after they had re-commenced reading the file and journal, Maria called. "Eddie, come here and look at this. Looks like our Sarah has been out and about! This entry here talks about Sarah needing special clothes for the yoga and the doctor notes that he had a nurse drive her to the mall so that she could get an all-black outfit. The nurse's report was that Sarah was very comfortable going to the mall and showed no nervousness at all. In fact, she noted that Sarah seemed to have a very good knowledge of the city."

"That must have been sometime in July as the file entries of July mention how Sarah was adjusting well to being given more responsibility in running the yoga classes which, apparently, were now fully booked. It also refers to the doctor's constant aim to have her fully integrated into society by the year end," Eddie added.

"Look here again," said Maria. "Another note about Sarah going for equipment for the classes. It doesn't say how or where she went. Let me read on and see if I can locate any more references before I say what I am thinking!"

When they had finished reading they both just looked at each other and simultaneously said "Are you thinking what I'm thinking?"

"I think the doctor stepped over the line in one way or another," Eddie began. "In his effort to build up the patient's confidence, he seems to have broken a lot of basic rules. For one, it would appear that he encouraged Sarah to go into the city, at first under the care of a nurse but then it would seem that later on he allowed her to take his car and go on her own. This has to be looked into. What was she doing? Who did she visit? Who in the clinic knew about this? So many questions to be answered. Not to mention, why he did it."

"From reading the journal, it appears to me that she became infatuated by him and one thing led to another, intentional or otherwise, and basically she seems to have had him around her little finger." Maria suggested. "Another thing, this explains Beth's claim that she had seen Tom's car on a number of occasions."

"I know that the Chief is away today but will be back in the morning. We need to show him what we have found and see what he suggests should be our next move. In the meantime, we say nothing to Beth, but we need to hold on to the files and journal."

Chapter 50

Eddie was just finished showering and dressing for his date when his cell phone buzzed.

"Eddie, sit down," said Shirley. "You won't believe it! Sarah Silver is none other than Alice Newman."

"What are you saying?"

"Just what I said – Sarah Silver is Alice Newman. I know she looks a little different from all the photos I have seen, but I am one hundred per cent certain that the lady who calls herself Sarah Silver and runs the yoga classes is Alice Newman."

"But this is mad. Are you sure?"

"The minute I met her I recognized her and what is more I believe that when she saw my reaction, she knew that I knew."

"So what happened next? What did you do?" asked a very shocked Eddie.

"Just for that second I could see it in her eyes and then as if a curtain closed, she regained her composure and acted as if nothing had passed between us. I pretended not to notice and muttered something stupid about having expected the coach to be a much older person. Anyway, I got a quick demonstration from there on – a fifteen-minute demonstration followed by her telling me that there were no places available until next year." said Shirley.

"Shirley I never doubted you before but this time you have surpassed my wildest expectations! However, I think that this bombshell is going to ruin our game tonight. See you in fifteen minutes Babe." said Eddie.

Once they had finished with their reunion hugs and kisses, which took some time since they hadn't seen each other for almost two weeks, Shirley having been working on a project two hundred miles west of Oldtown, Eddie said, "Now you can go to Butch and show him how really good you are. You now have an exclusive on the disappearance of Alice Newman. However, before you do that, first thing in the morning, I need to arrange a meeting with the Chief and the DA. Putting together what Maria and I have found yesterday and now this revelation has huge implications. We need to tread carefully and we need to prove with absolute certainty that Sarah Silver is Alice Newman – not that I doubt you for one second."

"Now let's forget about all that nasty business and enjoy ourselves. God how I missed you and your quirky humour. Just looking at you makes me feel so good." said Eddie, as they headed off to the ball game.

The next morning Eddie was waiting outside the

Chief's office when he arrived. "Good morning Eddie," said the Chief, "you look like the cat that got the cream. What have you resolved now?"

"Well actually I haven't resolved anything – yet. As a matter of fact, you could go so far as to say that I may have unsolved something." Eddie replied.

"That sounds ominous. What have you done?" the Chief grunted.

"Firstly, as you know, we have been following up on Doctor Mitchum's accident on behalf of his widow. This has led us to examine the doctor's life in more detail. It transpired that some years ago he took an interest in the court procedures for committing patients to psychiatric facilities on behalf of their families and monitoring their progress. He discovered patients who were, in his opinion, entitled to a review by the courts. When he followed up on ten of these cases the court ruled, having consulted the families in question, that there were no grounds for a review of their cases. However, in one case, that of a patient named Sarah Silver, he discovered that, other than the committal order signed by a judge up on Broadway, who had since died, there was absolutely no other documentation in the file. According to the clinic, she had no known relatives. Well the doctor appealed to the State Governor's office to have her released into his care at the Minerva Clinic here in the city, pending a full investigation of her case."

"So what is the relevance of all that to what we have been doing?" the Chief sighed, beginning to lose interest.

"This is where it gets interesting Chief. I mentioned yesterday, we located a file on this Sarah Silver in the doctor's briefcase and also a personal journal. From both of those we were able to see that the doctor spent an awful lot of time and energy in getting her back to health. However, in doing so he appears to have, in some ways, crossed ethical lines."

"Are you saying that he had an affair with the patient?"

"No, not really, but he did appear to compromise himself in his attempt, a successful attempt, to bring her back to health. His methods included getting her to reconnect with society by initially bringing her out for walks and following that up with getting her to visit the local mall in the care of a nurse in order to buy items for herself and the clinic yoga classes which she runs. Eventually he allowed her to borrow his car and go to the city on her own."

"But that seems to me, at the very least, to be in breach of the committal order not to mention any code of practice that the clinic should have." Said the Chief.

"Exactly," said Eddie, "But wait for the punch-line – we now have reason to believe that this Sarah Silver is in actual fact none other than, Alice Newman, Gregg

Newman's ex-wife."

"What?"

"What is right!" said Eddie. "If all of this is true, and we need to confirm the patient's identity, it would mean that Alice Newman was committed against her will by either her ex-husband, or persons' unknown, and under questionably grounds. It would then show a light on Newman's contention that there was a third party involved in the death of the babysitter. It would really open up a Pandora's box, don't you think?" said Eddie.

"It certainly would," the Chief mused. "How sure are you of these facts, Eddie?"

"The file and journal speak for themselves, the identity of the patient needs to be confirmed conclusively. At the moment I only have the opinion of someone I trust and who is exceptionally good at identifying people."

"That's good enough for me," the Chief responded. "Hold on while I see if Mary Donnelly is free. This is a definite job for the DA's office to rule on." When he was finished talking to Mary on the phone he said, "She will be with us in about ten minutes. Let's get some coffee and go back over what you have told me. It is like something out of a thriller. We could be talking about conspiracy to deny a person her freedom and unlawful confinement."

"But more than that, it opens up Newman's defense

that a car, resembling the doctor's car was seen in the vicinity of Newman's house and that a person, wearing black clothes, was also seen in the vicinity," Eddie reasoned. "This woman, whoever she is, bought an all-black outfit, for yoga. Also she was given the use of the doctor's car on a number of occasions."

They were just finished their coffee when Mary arrived.

"Ok, what have you got that is so important that I have had to come here immediately?" she snapped.

"I think you had better fill her in Eddie. We can then decide where we go from here." said the Chief.

After Eddie had recapped on the main points and Mary had quizzed him upside down on the facts and how he had ascertained them, Mary said, "The first thing we must do is to establish the true identity of the patient. To do this we need to consult with the clinic and get their permission to question the woman. Until we do this, the rest is pure speculation."

Chapter 51

It was decided that, due to the sensitivity of the situation, that Mary Donnelly would approach the clinic with the request to see and interview Sarah Silver, on the basis that as Doctor Mitchum was deceased she would have to be put under the care of another specified psychiatrist, in order to comply with the court committal order that still existed.

Matron Smyth was more than anxious to have this situation regularized at the earliest convenience and agreed to meet the DA that evening. On arriving at the clinic the DA, was shown in to the boardroom where Matron Smyth together with her assistant matron, Mis Starling, and an unidentified young man with a bushy beard, were waiting.

"Welcome to our clinic, District Attorney," said matron. "This is my assistant Miss Starling, I think you met her last year at our fundraiser, and this gentleman is our senior house psychiatrist, Doctor Power. He replaces the late Doctor Mitchum."

"Thank you, I am sure that this is only a formality," the DA began. "Once I have had sight of the patient and checked a few things with her, we can agree to Doctor Power taking over responsibility for her."

"Before we call Miss Silver in, is there anything in

particular we should know?" Matron asked.

"No, not really. We just need to know that we have the right person and that she is being looked after well. Just basic stuff."

Turning to Miss Starling, matron said, "Would you please bringing tihe patient in?"

"Please take a seat, Sarah," said matron, as Sarah, not making eye contact with anyone, almost crept in to the room with her head bowed. In appearance, a very fragile woman without a shred of makeup on her pale white face. "This is Mary Donnelly, our District Attorney who just wants to appoint a replacement doctor for you, now that poor Doctor Mitchum is no longer with us."

"There is no need to be nervous, Sarah." began the DA. "We just want to make sure you have the best support to help you journey back to the outside world as speedily as possible. I understand that under Doctor Mitchum's guidance, you have made remarkable progress and I must say that you look the picture of good health." (Even though she looked anything but the picture of health.)

"Thank you," said Sarah in a quiet voice.

"Tell me, are you happy to be located here in the Minerva Clinic or would you prefer to go back to the Haven Clinic?" Mary asked.

"Oh no, I am very happy here. I feel that it was only when I arrived here that I began to make any kind of progress. I don't want to leave here."

"I see, and I understand that as part of Doctor Mitchum's treatment, you ventured out to the city on a number of occasions. Is that right Sarah?"

If Mary had thrown a bomb on to the table, it wouldn't have caused as much consternation. Matron looked at Sarah. Miss Starling looked at matron and Doctor Power looked startled. Sarah looked at nobody.

"Well Sarah isn't that so? Was it traumatic, driving around a strange city?" the DA persisted.

"I'm not quite sure to what you are referring." said matron.

"All I want to know matron, is how Sarah felt to be back in the real world. A simple question surely. So once again Sarah, how was it?"

"I felt very nervous." Sarah whispered.

"But after the first few times I understand that you took to the one-way streets like a professional. Doctor Mitchum appeared to have been very excited at your progress." Mary continued.

Both matron and her assistant sat ashen-faced as they listened to Mary's questions. This was not what they had expected.

"Tell me Sarah, that is your name isn't it? Sarah Silver? Can you tell me where you were living before being committed to the clinic in Broadway?" the DA asked.

Again the question was met with silence as Sarah fidgeted with her fingers.

"You really must answer these questions, Sarah."

"No, I don't remember anything until this year when Doctor Mitchum worked with me. I only have short-term memory apparently." Sarah replied hesitantly, as she lifted a glass of water to take a drink.

Just as she was about to take a drink, Mary asked, "Does the name Gregg Newman mean anything to you Sarah?"

With that, Sarah, as her face turned a whiter shade of white, dropped the glass spilling the water all over her.

"Oh, I see you do have a long term memory after all. Why don't you tell us about it?" Mary said.

"I really must call a halt to this form of questioning," matron interrupted. "Can't you see how upset Sarah is? She will have to get out of those wet clothes as soon as possible. We can arrange for a further session at another time."

"Sorry matron, but this is very important. I just have one more question for Sarah and then we can take a break so that she can change out of her wet clothes. Tell me, what is your real name?"

"Matron knows that I am Sarah Silver." replied Sarah, looking away.

"I know that as far as the clinic is concerned," the DA countered, "that you are registered here as Sarah Silver. Before you answer, be aware that we know a lot about you Sarah. I just want to hear you admit it."

Chapter 52

The silence in the room was electric. Everyone stared at Sarah, not knowing what to expect. The interview had gone down a road that no one knew anything about, or had expected. Finally, in a very quiet voice, Sarah replied, "My name is Alice Newman."

"Thank you," said the DA. "That changes a lot of things. We know that you have an ex-husband who is now serving a jail sentence. We also know that you have an eight-year-old daughter, Tracey, isn't that true? Your ex-husband was given custody of her at your divorce hearing."

"My God," said matron, "where does all of this leave us?"

"Now Alice, the police are outside and are waiting to come in to interview you in connection with your breach of the conditions of your committal order. They also have a warrant to immediately search your room." Since Alice was a private patient, the warrant was issued in the name of Alice Newman also, known as Sarah Silver.

It was Eddie's suggestion that the room be searched immediately in the hope that they might find something that would connect Alice to Mr Newman's recent case or to the accident that killed Doctor Mitchum. Turning to the shocked matron she said, "As soon as I return to my office I will initiate a full and comprehensive investigation into your committal. In the meantime, Sarah, sorry I mean Alice, is to remain here in your care but confined to the clinic as she should always have been."

"This is absurd," shouted a very different and very angry, Alice Newman. "You are trampling on my rights. I want a lawyer, now!"

"Yes Alice, we will arrange that for you. In the meantime, matron you might be good enough to bring in the officers who will interview Ms Newman."

When Eddie and Maria were ushered into to the boardroom they were met by an aggressive Ms Newman.

"What is this all about?" she cried, trying to barge her way out of the room. "You have no right to do this. I want a lawyer."

"Sorry Miss, but we do have the right to question you and to search your room. You can discuss all of this with the lawyer the court will allocate to you in the morning," said Eddie, "Now please take a seat. We only want to find out the truth."

As soon as Alice was seated at the boardroom table she again demanded that the search of her room be stopped.

"I'm afraid we can't do that Ms Newman, not in the middle of an investigation. Right now we need to ask you some questions. Questions in relation to your ex-husband's recent court case." said Eddie.

"Let's start at the beginning Alice. Tell us how you ended up being committed to the Haven Clinic." Maria began.

"I now remember having a very public spat with my husband. I had a lot to drink that night and accused him in public of certain things. The next thing I remember was being dragged away and our doctor injecting me with something. What happened to me after that is a complete haze. I remember waking up in a strange place. Nobody would listen to me; they just kept on giving me sedation again and again and calling me Sarah. They told me I was insane and that a court had had me committed because of my behaviour and hallucinations about having a husband and a child. Eventually I must have believed what they were saying. I began to doubt my own reason."

"So when Doctor Mitchum met you, did you have any idea of what he was talking about?" Eddie intervened.

"No, at that stage I just wanted to die. I had no idea what was coming as long as I got my tablets. They erased the pain and confusion. Then the doctor started withdrawing the tablets. Apparently they were exceptionally strong and addictive. It was only after a few months of coming off them slowly that I began to think again. Doctor Tom was so kind and gentle. He didn't deserve to die."

"Do you have any idea why he died?" asked Eddie.

"I think that it was his kindness that killed him. He didn't have to take my pain on himself – but he did. As I began to relive what my husband had done to me and my daughter – he lived that pain with me. He suffered from high blood pressure but never told his wife. When he would allow me to visit the city in his car so that I could look at my daughter, from a distance, I knew it took so much out of him. Yet he knew how important it was for me and so he endured that pressure every time. He knew that if he was found out he could lose his job. But he knew that his job was to repair me and save me."

"Tell me where you went to look at your daughter and where else did you go, on those excursions into the city, Alice?" Maria continued.

"Initially I would do some shopping for bits and pieces and some clothes for myself. Doctor Tom would suggest that I spend some of his money on an outfit, just to lift my spirits, as he would say. However, as I mentioned, my main reason would be to catch sight of my daughter. You have no idea of the pain it caused for me to watch her with him and not to be able to touch her or talk to her. The bastard." Alice almost spat those last words.

"Did you ever go near Mr Newman's home?" Eddie asked.

"You mean my home! Of course I did, I needed to be able to walk around every inch of my bedroom, my kitchen, my everything. It was mine and will always be mine." Alice snapped.

"But how did you get into the house, Alice?"

"From watching the house and knowing that Gregg never changed his habits, I knew that he would be using the same alarm code that he always used. It was only a matter of finding a way in."

"So how did you gain access?"

"I followed Gregg on his Friday jog a few times and noticed that while he always went in to our house by the front door, he always left by the back entrance. I then noticed him planting something in the wall by the back entrance. When he had gone I checked and found that he had hidden a set of keys in the wall. I took them and had a set cut for myself. It was that easy."

Chapter 53

"Getting back to the evening you were taken away from the Country Club. Do you remember who was involved in you being committed to the clinic?"

"Well, the full Election Committee were there at the meeting. It was that meeting I gate-crashed. I remember our own doctor, Doctor Jim Mackey, and our attorney, Al McNally, were involved in getting me out of the Club and into hospital. After that it is all very vague in my mind. I kept screaming for Gregg to get me out but now I know it was what he wanted. I was surplus to requirements as far as he was concerned. It soon dawned on me that no one was going to help me. Then I began to forget everything and believe that I was Sarah. It was only in the last year, thanks to Doctor Tom that I became aware that I had been divorced and lost my daughter. I nearly relapsed into insanity but that would have suited Gregg and so I adopted the motto 'Don't get angry, get even'. That kept me going on many a long hopeless day. Now I must insist on my rights to have a lawyer present before I answer any further questions." said Alice adamantly.

"Thanks, Alice. You have been most helpful. We must see what has to be done next. We will call again tomorrow to continue our interview, as soon as your lawyer is appointed."

When they got back to the station they found the Chief and DA ensconced in the Chief's office with Lennie Bareman from the forensic team. "Bring another chair Eddie. This office was never built for five people." the Chief called out.

"Just to recap," the Chief continued, "Lennie has given us his report on the search of the patient's room. Firstly, he found, well-hidden at the bottom of her wardrobe, a number of booklets on Taser guns and on how to use them effectively. He also found a number of instruction booklets on surveillance cameras and a significant number of computer printouts relating to car engines, specifically on how power steering and braking systems work. He also found a supply of pills of all shapes and sizes. We have sent them for analysis. Also in the box were a number of house keys, latex gloves and a black ski mask. Finally, he found her cell phone and looking through her camera record he found numerous photos of Gregg Newman's house and of his daughter, some on her own and others with Mr Newman."

"Pretty conclusive I would say," Eddie agreed, "and it ties in with what we discovered during our interview with her. It appears that when Alice realized what had happened, and that was only in the past six months, she stalked Newman to the extent of visiting his, or as she maintains – her home. On one occasion she watched him hide a set of keys to the lane and back doors, apparently for the babysitter. She had these keys copied and after that she apparently wandered in and out of the house as she pleased. She knew the alarm would be off and even if it wasn't, she knew the alarm code and also the code to the safe. It was always Mr Newman's date of birth. Gregg Newman was a creature of habit and used the same code always."

"So what was she up to?" asked the Chief.

"I don't know exactly," Eddie answered. "She was very anxious to see her daughter but was afraid that if Tracey saw her, she might tell Newman and he would have her back in Broadway. This way she was anonymous, with Newman thinking she was safely tucked away up in Broadway. She could move around freely and plan some sort of revenge."

"Hold on," said the DA, "before we tie ourselves in knots, let's review the situation. In the first instance, Gregg Newman was acquitted of the death of the babysitter. So he can't be charged again. He is serving a sentence for statutory rape and that stands.

Secondly, Alice Newman is still incarcerated under

court order and has, with the encouragement and permission of the doctor, who took responsibility for her incarceration broken that court ruling.

Thirdly, her doctor, Doctor Mitchum, died in an extraordinary accident (The cause of which was never fully discovered) on the very day that the babysitter died in Newman's home.

However, for me, the main issue is the apparent conspiracy to incarcerate Alice Newman in a psychiatric facility. The objective of which it would appear, was to ensure that nothing stopped the Democratic Party from having their man, Gregg Newman, as the next mayor. If we are to believe what Alice has said, then this conspiracy involved a number of people, Gregg Newman, Doctor Jim Mackey his doctor, Al McNally his attorney, and others."

"So it is the word of a committed psychiatric patient against these 'pillars of society'. I don't think we would have a hope in hell of getting a conviction." The Chief commented.

"Maybe not, but that shouldn't stop us from trying," interjected Eddie, "Let's look for the weakest link in that chain. What has Gregg to lose; he is finished as a politician in this town, and washed out by the Party. I also know that he is finding his new accommodation difficult to adjust to, and what of the doctor up in Broadway who for all of that time administered the treatment to Alice. But now, thanks to Doctor Mitchum, we know that it was excessive and unethical. He could be vulnerable to a little pressure, perhaps?"

"Good thinking Eddie, that's an excellent idea. If the doctor would crack even a little, we will have something to proceed with. Check him out and then get an interview with Newman, but don't offer him anything in return. Not yet."

Chapter 54

As soon as Eddie left the office he rang Matron Smyth. "Hi matron, sorry to bother you again so soon but I am wondering if you could help me. We are anxious to talk to the doctor up in Broadway who administered the medication to Alice. Have you any way of finding out who he is and how he could be contacted? It is very important that we speak to him."

"Certainly detective," she replied, "We are still in a state of shock here and of course anything we can do to help, we will. Give me time to contact my colleague in Broadway and I am sure that he will be able to tell me."

Twenty minutes later Matron Smyth called back. "This is most strange. The doctor in question is a retired doctor who was never actually attached to the clinic but who, for some unknown reason that nobody can tell, had been given responsibility for Alice's medication. He lives about twenty miles south of Broadway in a little country town. I will fax you his full details. This is most unusual. I have never heard of anything like it before."

While he was waiting for the fax to come through,

Eddie called the prison Governor to arrange an interview with Newman. He then called Shirley and told her that he would have to cancel their lunch date for the following day as he had to go back up to Broadway but would be free for dinner that evening if she was free. "Is this just another delay in getting the painting done?" was her opening quip. "I don't know how you make up such weak excuses, Detective Eddie McGrane."

"What I didn't tell you, my Darling, is that, as I will be heading off at the crack of dawn tomorrow. I intend packing up here in the next few minutes and then going straight back to the apartment to finish the painting of the kitchen. As promised, it will be ready for you to move in next Saturday. By the way, I will have a lot to tell you about your missing lady," he added.

When the fax finally came through, Eddie brought it in to the Chief who still had the DA with him. "This is the guy, Doctor Quentin Moody, who was responsible for Alice up in Broadway. Dear God, he looks as if he is as old as Methuselah, he must be ninety if he is a day. Also I am told that he was never officially attached to the clinic but had, somehow, been appointed to medicate Alice. This should be interesting. We are heading up there first thing in the morning and intend to surprise him. I hope he will still be alive when I get there." Eddie joked.

It was mid-morning when they eventually pulled in to the address they had been given. The house, on its own grounds, smelt of wealth. It had its own swimming pool set amid beautiful landscaped gardens. Certainly not a house that was short of money.

"Good morning, doctor," said Eddie, as they were met on the doorstep by a sprightly old man whom Eddie immediately recognized from the photo he had received from matron. "My name is Detective Eddie McGrane and this is my partner, Officer Maria Diego, we would like to ask you a few questions, if you don't mind?"

"What is this in connection with?" he said cautiously, "Have I been speeding again?"

"Well it is a long story and not a speeding one, I can assure you. Do you mind if we come in?" Eddie replied.

"Certainly. Oh sorry. I forgot my manners. Do come in."

When they were seated Eddie explained, "Before we start we would like to record our discussion if you have no objection."

"No, that's ok with me," he replied, again looking suspiciously at both of them.

"Now, you asked us what this is about. Well we hope you can clear up something for an investigation that we are involved in. During our investigation your name came up in connection with a lady whose name is, Alice or Becky Newman, does that name mean anything to you?"

"No, I'm afraid I have never heard of those names," the doctor replied defensively.

"How about Sarah Silver? Have you ever heard of her?" asked Maria.

"Sarah Silver? Why does that name seem familiar to me? I seem to recall something about that name…" a now visibly flustered Doctor Moody responded.

"Yes you should well remember that name," Eddie warned. "You treated her in the Haven Clinic up in Broadway for a number of years. What we now want to know is who paid you to do that? Your cooperation will save you a lot of grief doctor."

"I don't know what you are talking about officer. And even if I did," said the doctor, "I am constrained by doctor and patient confidentiality."

"Listen doctor and listen well. We are investigating a very serious conspiracy case. And we are not asking you to breach confidence between you and a patient. We just want you to tell us who it was that instructed you. Be aware that if you refuse to cooperate with us, we will have no other option but to have you called up before a Grand Jury. You could face a jail sentence for obstruction of justice. Now, once more, who was it, please?"

"What will happen to me if I tell you?"

"We can't say, but let me assure you it will be a lot less than if you don't tell us. We are after those who set this up. You are only one of the operators of the scheme. One of the small fry."

Finally, the doctor broke down and admitted everything. Over the years he had developed a very serious gambling problem. A problem that necessitated him hurriedly leaving his very senior position in the nearby State General Hospital. It also ended his ten-year-old marriage. He had relocated to Wayward where he resided in a one-bedroom apartment for a few years. One day he was surprised when a doctor from a place called Oldtown, Doctor Jim Mackey, personally called to see him. He said he had a problem and wanted the doctors' help to solve it. He told him that he sympathized with his position, which he said he knew all about, and his problems would go away. He was to look after a patient of his who had been relocated to the Broadway clinic. All he had to do was ensure that she was fully and constantly sedated until she doubted her own reason. Her name was Sarah Silver. In return, the monies he owed his own bank would be written off and in addition, he would be paid handsomely by monthly bank order drawn on a bank in Oldtown, the same bank that had a monthly payment paid to the clinic.

"You do however know that Sarah was moved to another clinic almost two years ago, don't you? Did you not wonder why your monthly payments stopped?" Maria asked.

"But they never stopped. I still receive the payment every third Thursday of the month. I assumed that they appreciated my keeping my mouth shut about it all," the doctor explained.

"You are probably right doctor. We are sure they would have liked to cover their tracks completely. However, they obviously underestimated the resilience of two women – Sarah Silver and a young cub TV reporter who discovered her true identity."

Chapter 55

As soon as they got back to the car, Eddie rang the Chief, and told him what they had found out and that they were now heading back and would be calling to the prison to interview Newman. He then rang the prison Governor to advise him of their estimated time of arrival.

Ninety minutes later they were in the Governor's office having a well-deserved coffee.

"So you want to interview Gregg Newman again." The Governor began, "Is there a doubt over his conviction? I know that he has already launched a number of appeals, and of course, having regard to the nature of his crime, he is not very popular with the other prisoners."

"No, this is just to clear up a few issues that arose during the trial." Eddie replied.

"Fine, come with me so. Newman is already in the interview room. You do of course realize that your interview will be recorded, is that ok?" The Governor reminded him.

"No problem at all." Eddie replied, "We'll be recording it also."

"Good afternoon Mr Newman," said Eddie, as they

sat in the bare interview room, opposite a very shattered looking Newman. His stay in the prison hadn't been kind to him, "I hope they are treating you here, as you deserve."

"I want out of here, officer." said Newman. "This is outrageous. You know and I know that this is a travesty of justice. The jury were obviously bought. I was set up."

"Well now Mr Newman, I hate to tell you this but you might be in more trouble than you realize. As a matter of fact, I think you may be in here a lot longer than you think." Eddie responded.

"You must be joking! How did you come to that conclusion, officer?"

"Mr Newman, it has come to our attention that your wife – or ex-wife, disappeared very mysteriously some years ago and you claimed to have no knowledge of her whereabouts, or so you informed us, right?"

"Yes, we are divorced and she has not kept in contact with me since then."

"Sorry, Mr Newman, but we don't buy that story. We know the real story and before we go any further we want you to understand that you are facing a very long sentence for conspiracy to unlawfully detaining a person against her will. You conspired, with other parties to falsely commit your wife, against her will, to a psychiatric clinic. However, if you cooperate with us it may mitigate any sentence you may get. Your best bet would be to turn States Evidence and tell us exactly what happened to Alice."

Two hours later, Newman, having agreed to turn States Evidence, finished his evidence implicating three of the Election Committee members; Leo Forrest, Al McNally and Doctor Jim Mackey, in the unlawful detention of Alice Newman.

That evening the NTTV News, with reporter Shirley Green, speaking from outside the headquarters of the Democratic Party, and under the banner 'Breaking News' announced that three members of the Executive of the city's Democratic Party had been arrested for questioning in connection with the detention and false imprisonment of Ms Alice Newman, at a psychiatric facility. Ms Newman's ex-husband had been the Democratic candidate for the recent mayoral election and was currently serving a jail sentence on a sex charge.

The following morning, at a review meeting with the investigating team, once again in his Chief's small office, the Chief said, "Well done Eddie. I guess that wraps it up I think, but keep an eye on that itch of yours – it never lets you down! Now the next big question is what we do about

Ms Newman. From what she has admitted so far, it looks certain that she was very much involved in the event that took place the night that the babysitter died, doesn't it?"

"Yes it does, but to what extent was she involved? We also know that Newman was involved, but he was acquitted by a jury so we can't charge him again. In other words, we still don't know who killed Angie Lummox." said Eddie.

"Also it is important to remember, that whatever we may think or surmise, there is nothing we can charge Ms Newman with." interrupted the DA. "In law she is not responsible for any of her actions. A court has deemed her insane and until that order is rescinded, she remains legally insane."

The End

Retribution for Alice

'Retribution for Alice' by P.T. Chambers, is the explosive sequel to 'Has Anyone Seen Alice?'

Following on from Alice being declared legally insane, observe the unfolding courtroom drama, witness what happens to the accused and question what fate holds in store for the many players in this complex story of incarceration, revenge, loss and betrayal.

Follow Detective Eddie McGrane, his partner Maria Diego and the ever zealous rookie reporter Shirley Green as they try to piece everything together, working against the clock, and against very clever people who will stop at nothing to prevent the past from being exposed. And above all question the role Alice plays in all this chaos.

Dear Reader

I hope you enjoyed 'Has Anyone Seen Alice?'

As an author I love feedback. We are living in a wonderfully technological age, where you, the reader, have the power to influence discourse and have a say in how future books are written. Please do take the opportunity to let your voice be heard by contacting me directly or by following my blog via the links given below.
Email:ptchambers@eircom.net
Blog:ramblingsfromphilc.blogspot.ie
Thank you for reading!

P.T. Chambers

Made in the USA
Charleston, SC
07 July 2016